TERROR IN GUNSIGHT

Center Point
Large Print

Also by Lauran Paine and available from
Center Point Large Print:

Night of the Rustler's Moon
Iron Marshal
Six-Gun Crossroads
Dead Man's Cañon
Reckoning at Lansing's Ferry
The Drifter
Winter Moon
The Texan Rides Alone

**This Large Print Book carries the
Seal of Approval of N.A.V.H.**

TERROR IN GUNSIGHT

LAURAN PAINE

CENTER POINT LARGE PRINT
THORNDIKE, MAINE

This Circle Ⓥ Western is published by
Center Point Large Print in the year 2018 in
co-operation with Golden West Literary Agency.

First Edition
October 2018

The text of this Large Print edition is unabridged.
In other aspects, this book may vary
from the original edition.
Printed in the United States of America
on permanent paper.
Set in 16-point Times New Roman type.

ISBN: 978-1-68324-963-4

Library of Congress Cataloging-in-Publication Data

Names: Paine, Lauran, author.
Title: Terror in gunsight : a Circle V Western / Lauran Paine.
Description: First edition. | Thorndike, Maine :
    Center Point Large Print, 2018.
Identifiers: LCCN 2018028750 | ISBN 9781683249634
    (hardcover : alk. paper)
Subjects: LCSH: Large type books. | GSAFD: Western stories.
Classification: LCC PS3566.A34 T44 2018 | DDC 813/.54—dc23
LC record available at https://lccn.loc.gov/2018028750

CHAPTER ONE

He approached the rising rimrocks of the westerly plateau, pushed swiftly upward, and hurried along to the final lip of the drop-off. There, he paused only long enough to seek out a way directly downward into the jack pine and manzanita country below before urging his horse outward—and downward.

There was no trail here, not even deer used this perilous descent. It was too steep and barring the single long spine of narrow ridge leading downward, there was no other way off the rimrocks.

On either side of this stringy hogback of razor-like slope the terrain dropped precipitously away. He could easily see that one misstep meant a five-hundred-foot fall and certain death.

He had no choice. He knew pursuit was even now passing rapidly across the dished-out plateau behind, swinging eagerly up toward the rimrocks, confident he was brought to earth. If he had not taken the risk, he would have been easily enough surrounded among the rimrocks and shot to death. So he rode now, scarcely able to see his horse's head out front it was so far below him, with his hips jammed against the cantle and his booted feet thrust far forward to maintain balance that his spur rowels from time to time were even with his horse's sweaty ears.

He did not raise his eyes or deepen the sweep of breath into his lungs until, six hundred feet farther down off the dizzying heights, he could see that his horse's sure-footedness was going to bring him through this alive. Then he cast a searching, anxious glance out over the rise and fall of westerly countryside.

Where mountain flanks drew sharply back beyond this broken, scrub country, lay a broad, lush green valley. Around it, distantly purple in the midday sunlight, lay the encircling lift of still more mountains. The valley itself was sealed off by these monoliths from the rest of the world. It was a land unto itself.

Near the center of the valley he made out distantly the squares of reflected daylight off metal roofs of buildings, but the distance was far too great for him to be able to determine anything more than that what he saw out there was a town. Still, he told himself, that was enough. If he could reach that town, he would be safe. There would be a sheriff there, or a town marshal, or some kind of a lawman who would protect him from the four hard-riding strangers who had fired at him, and who had then chased him this far.

His horse began gradually to straighten up beneath the saddle. They were at last upon safe ground again. From here on, there was manzanita with its smooth red trunk coloring the flinty earth, and occasionally a patch or two of jack-pine shade. The animal's shoulder muscles quivered from exertion. Its hide was shiny with sweat and its distended nostrils showed their red-veined interior.

He did not use the spurs again, but let the horse seek out and find its own way through the sticker pointed scrub, which it did through employment of that mysterious sagacity in such matters which all horses have.

He was passing well along with only head and shoulders visible, when faintly came the flat smash of a single gunshot. He twisted to look back quickly. Overhead upon the very edge of the precipice, sat the four pursuing riders. They obviously had no stomach for following his trail downward from the rimrocks, and that one long-range shot said as much.

Around him the hot summer stillness bore down with an almost physical pressure. At least here in the breathless fold of eddying foothills there was no coolness, no little breeze or freshening scent. Beyond the last spread of out-falling land to the south where the valley began, there would be blessed coolness, for Wyoming's high country was never, even in the hottest of summers, without its succoring freshets of mountain air. These came down from perpetually snow-frosted crags above timberline in that season, and in the dark winter they froze the marrow in a man's bones. In summertime, too, they brought a fragrance, a freshness, and a lift.

He made for a small flinty knoll where a struggling red fir and an ancient, warped and twisted old juniper stood. There, he swung out and down, flung up the stirrup leather, tugged loose the latigo, and lifted the saddle for air to pass over his animal's heaving back. The horse expanded his lungs to their fullest, then let out that air with a great sighing sound. Slowly he moved his feet to stand hip-shot, gazing with quickening interest at this country round about which was new to both of them.

The rider hunkered moments later to make a cigarette, to light it, to inhale deeply, and turn his steady gray gaze outward as far as he could see. Behind him, where the rimrocks ran east and west, there was no abridging rib of land as far as he could see in either direction, excepting the one he had come by plunging downward. Since his pursuers had declined to use that one, he surmised, they would spend hours trying to find an easier and safer way of getting down out of those uplands.

So he smoked, studied the valley, and waited for his horse to recover from the miles-long run and the frightening last descent to safety.

It was, he thought, a beautiful and rich valley. Here, in the insular vastness of Wyoming's high country, the world beyond scarcely existed. A man might almost feel reborn here. Whatever of himself might lay beyond the mountains, he could leave forever behind. Even the pursuit by four outlaws seemed part of the tribulation a man must endure in order to achieve this place of rebirth.

Thinking like this, the horseman's spirit rose. His assurance returned, and he arose, eventually, to tug up the latigo, toe in, and rise up to settle across his saddle with a sense of peace coming to him.

He urged the horse ahead, riding a loose rein, letting his animal seek out and find its own way out of the thorny maze. He was in no hurry now, and in fact, after the custom of men inured to danger, he left all thought of the recent chase behind him as he passed beyond the final brushy fringe and emerged upon the valley floor.

He passed along comfortably now, riding loosely, considering the land, the distant mountains, the signs of life, and, here and there, the grazing small bands of dark red cattle.

This, he told himself, was a prosperous valley. Here, the people would know comfort, peace, and probably wealth. He had a theory about these things—an idea formed over his years as a rider. In a country where the soil was deep, the people were substantial. In a land where the top soil was poor or shallow or gritty, people were edgy, troublesome, and sometimes suspicious of strangers.

A weathered wooden sign with an arrow upon it pointing westerly, in the direction he was riding, had a single name upon it.

Gunsight

He smiled at that, for by raising his glance only slightly he saw dead ahead, far beyond the town of Gunsight, a diminishingly narrow notch in the faraway mountains. This particular type of a mountain pass was referred to by Westerners as a gunsight or a gunsight pass. It had required no imagination on the part of the citizenry, he thought, to name the valley's only town.

The silence, the timelessness, and the peacefulness which seemed to abide in this place, worked its subtle magic, and with the town of Gunsight well in view, perhaps twenty or thirty minutes away, he drew up again, this time in the filigree shade of creek willows, and dismounted. He was in no hurry, had never in his life been in any hurry for that matter. The grass here was darkly luxuriant, his animal was hungry, there was a hurrying little narrow creek low in the grass, and there was the shade. No range man ever overlooked so inviting an opportunity to tarry a moment when such an enticing combination of conditions was present. He let the horse wander, dragging the reins, while he himself dropped down in the shade, pushed long legs out to their limit, tilted forward his hat brim, and settled back, his body going loose in the warmth of the afternoon. He was a little bothered by hunger. He had not eaten since dawn, on the sundown side of the mountains. But again, to a man accustomed to inconvenience, this was not a very important thing. He would eat in Gunsight.

For a while the only sounds came from his eating horse and the little creek. Then, vaguely heard at first, but gradually coming on, there was the rapid pacing forward of ridden horses. He pushed back his hat to cast an indifferent but curious glance northward—then stiffened. Even at that distance he recognized the same four outlaws who had earlier pursued him.

For a moment he was astonished, for although bands of bandits infested Wyoming's mountains, he had never before heard of any as bold as these men. They were coming almost to the very outskirts of Gunsight itself, in their search for victims.

He arose, moving swiftly, caught his animal, and swung up into the saddle. He then reined across the creek and started along the far bank beyond a screening of willows, toward town. He did not, right then, have any premonition of disaster. In fact, gauging the distance between his pursuers and himself, he knew he could reach

Gunsight well ahead of his enemies, because, although they were obviously hunting him, they were still a long mile away.

Where the creek ultimately veered southward he was compelled to ride clear of his cover. He was then less than a mile from town. Behind, came the faintly echoing shout of a pursuer. Over his shoulder he saw the four men converge, after sighting him, then urge their mounts onward through dazzling sunlight, rushing headlong after him. Because he was now at the outer extremity of Gunsight and felt completely safe, he reined up to briefly sit and consider. Never before in his experience had he ever even heard of, let alone encountered, such bold outlaws. He shrugged. The law at Gunsight must be very tolerant, he thought. His brother had once told him . . .

A crashing gunshot shattered this reverie and he lingered no longer but pushed ahead into the town of Gunsight.

Situated nearly in the exact center of the valley, Gunsight was a log, board-and-batten village with one very wide main avenue and a number of random side roads. At either end of town stood a large saloon, evidently placed there by calculating proprietors who assumed that the best place for business was where people either entered or left town. Between these establishments on either side of the central roadway, were opposite ranks of stores, shops, and offices. Near the middle of town on the south side was the livery barn. Directly across from the barn was a freshly painted log building with the legend: **Drovers' and Cattlemen's Restaurant** emblazoned across its front. This, rather than either of the widely separated saloons, appeared to be the popular gathering spot for idlers. He guessed this was perhaps due to the only shade tree for the full length of Gunsight's central roadway, which stood here, and around its enormous bole had been constructed several benches.

As the tall, young cowboy scuffed through midday's hot dust to draw up and swing down in front of the livery barn, a number of idlers seated beneath this tree ceased speaking and turned motionless for the length of time it took to appraise him, his horse, and the equipment carried by both. Finally, a raw-boned man with his Barlow knife in one fist and part of a whittled stick in the other hand, arose wordlessly, snapped the knife closed, pocketed it, and went ambling carelessly through the sun smash toward a dark and gloomy log building which bore the single word, **Sheriff**, over its doorway.

At the livery barn another man, older, shorter, less grim in the face, came out to take the young rider's reins and gaze uncomfortably into his face.

The cowboy said: "Better cool him out. I had to run him a little beyond town." He did not mention the pursuing four horsemen and only shrugged when the liveryman also spoke.

"Pretty hot for fast riding, stranger."

"I didn't have much choice." The cowboy turned to run a considering gaze along the roadway. "Where's a good place to eat?"

The liveryman stood there running the reins through his fingers nervously without replying. His gaze was fixed fully upon two men angling across toward him from the direction of the sheriff's office. His face paled and he made a quick circuit of his lips with the tip of his tongue.

The cowboy faced back, faintly frowning. Words were upon his lips, but he did not utter them. The liveryman's expression kept him silent. Following out the liveryman's stare, he saw both approaching men. He watched as the hard slam of their booted feet raised up little puffs of dun dust from the roadway. Within him something instinctive stirred. Some intuitive warning flashed along his nerves.

Then the two men stopped, one moving sideways away from the other, older man. The faces of both men were tough-set and resolute. In that moment the rider recognized the imminence of peril. When two men went up against another armed man, they did not stand together for the elemental reason that by forcing their adversary to shift position in order to fire twice, he could not hope to shoot both men.

The older man then spoke. His voice was without inflection, and it was deadly.

"Unbuckle that gun belt and let it fall," he ordered, not for a second taking his eyes off the young cowboy.

Behind them, across the roadway, idlers at the benches around the cottonwood tree, began moving well out of any line of fire. Northerly too, came the slowly paced movement of four red-faced men riding fully abreast. These, the cowboy saw at once, were the same four who had pursued him. The same four who had fired at him and who he had never for a moment doubted were out-laws. They now ranged themselves, still astride, behind the sheriff and his afoot companion, training upon the cowboy four cocked revolvers.

"I said let that gun belt fall!" the older man ordered again.

There was no alternative to obedience. The gun belt fell into the dust, making its own soft rustling sound, as the cowboy said: "I don't know what this is all about." He sounded genuinely bewildered.

From one of the horsemen came the flinty words: "I reckon you don't at that. I reckon you didn't expect us to be ready like this."

"Ready for what? What are you talking about?" asked the cowboy.

"About hired killers," said the grizzled, thin-lipped and deadly eyed sheriff. "I reckon you figured you'd just ride in, shoot whoever you've come to kill, then ride out again. By God, stranger," went on that cold voice after a brief pause, "you made the biggest mistake of your life coming to Gunsight." The sheriff relaxed a little, tilting back his head and staring bleakly down his nose. "What's your name, gunfighter?"

"I'm no gunfighter," protested the young cowboy.

"What's your damned name, I asked!"

"Pete Knight."

"Come on, Pete Knight," growled the sheriff. "I got a special cell for your kind."

CHAPTER TWO

"Hobart sent for him," said an idler under the cottonwood tree. "I'll lay money on it."

There were five of them sitting there in the shade. The man who had spoken was chewing tobacco and leaning with his shoulders against the tree trunk. He had both fisted hands shoved deeply into pockets. His eyes were pinched nearly closed.

"Hobart's going to continue bossing this country if he has to hire himself a dozen gunfighters."

A wizened man with skin the color of old wood, said simply: "He'll be fightin' mad when he hears us townspeople corralled his gunfighter."

"Let him get mad," snarled a third man, looking grimly at the piece of wood he was whittling. "He don't own this town."

"He thinks he does. He sure as the devil owns everything else in the valley."

"But not the town."

A heretofore silent man said: "They ought to tar and feather that there gunfighter."

"They ought to lynch him," said another idler, speaking up strongly. "That's what they ought to do. Hobart's men have rid roughshod over folks hereabouts too damned long. It's about time one of 'em was made an example of."

The leaning man turned his pinched down eyes to stare at this last speaker. He withdrew his fisted hands and folded them in his lap, fingers intertwined. After an ensuing moment of silence, he said: "You're plumb right, August. He ought to be lynched and we ought to have a celebration after it's accomplished."

This thought, with its ugly implications, held all of them silent for a long time. A man who had taken no part in this discussion at all so far, scratched his jaw, spat amber liquid into the roadway dust, and arose. "Been an awful lot o' talk!" he exclaimed shortly. "And nothin' but talk." He studied the other men sitting with him beneath the big cottonwood tree. "Any you fellows ever seen a lynching?"

No one replied. Every head had dropped into a low position, eyes were averted, but they were carefully listening now.

"I have," said the narrow-faced standing man. "I helped pull the rope."

Someone quietly asked: "What had he done?"

"Stoled a horse," replied the standing man. "But he was a gunfighter, too. Where I come from . . . we took care of them kind right quick."

Silence settled again. The only sound was the buzzing of the blue-tailed flies. The town around them dozed in midday somnolence. A horseman jogged past, heading northward. No one even looked up.

Finally, a man said: "Seems kind of young for a gunfighter."

"Mostly they are young," stated the standing man, implying with his crispness a great knowledge of gunfighters. "Mostly, too, they don't none of 'em live to get much older."

"Good thing folks heard that rumor of his coming," someone said.

The leaning man, long silent in a thoughtful way, now straightened up off the tree trunk. "Sheriff Mike can't hold him. He ain't killed no one yet. You got to have charges to hold a man in jail."

"Yeah," mumbled someone. "And when he turns him loose . . . then what?"

The standing man had an answer for this. He said: "He'll go see Hobart, get his blood money and a name . . . then maybe tomorrow or the next day someone from town gets bushwhacked. Then the gunfighter rides on with his money, plumb safe . . . and we got to bury someone."

"About this lynching business," a man said now. "Sheriff Mulaney had likely not go along with it." Someone snorted in reponse, but the man continued: "He ain't going to put up much of an argument. Not Mike. He's sicker than most of us of all this squabbling with Hobart's Diamond H cow outfit." After a pause followed by silence

19

among the others, this same man added: "I'll bet five, six fellows could walk in on Mike tonight with masks on, throw down on him, take that danged murderer out of his cell, and lynch him, and Mike wouldn't say a word."

The standing man spread wide his legs and leaned back to gaze upward. "This here tree," he stated with knowledgeable force, "is just exactly right for a lynching."

Nearly a full minute passed before the slit-eyed man with the folded hands got to his feet and said: "Well . . . ?"

The others, excepting the standing man, shifted where they sat. Two who were whittling, peeled off longer slivers with their knives, indications of troubled thoughts, then one of them closed his knife with sharp finality and also arose.

"I'm with you," he said softly.

Seconds ticked away. They arose to stand resolutely, one by one. The last man to arise was the wizened, weathered man whose mahogany hide gave him an appearance of having Indian blood. He carefully pouched a cud of chewing tobacco, saying to the others: "We got to go somewhere and plan this. We can't stand around here talking, it's too dangerous."

"Behind the blacksmith shed out back of the livery barn," a man said, beginning to move away. "But make it look casual-like. Can't take no chances."

Several uneasy glances were bent upon the front of Sheriff Mike Mulaney's office. There was nothing down there to see. The door was closed, sunlight glittered against the one small barred window, and there was no horse at Mulaney's hitch rail.

In fact, all of Gunsight seemed to be indoors. A bonneted woman passed into Blakely's Emporium, basket on her arm. And then the length of the plank walk was empty.

In the livery barn doorway, a hostler lounged, arms crossed, brown-paper cigarette dead between his lips. In the recessed entrance to Howell's saddlery old Jacob Howell himself sat in an old cane-bottomed chair that was wired together, tilted back against the wood-work, drowsing. Old Jacob had come to Gunsight before there had been a town there at all. He had once been a beaver trapper and mountain man.

The door of Mulaney's office opened inward. It was a purposefully reinforced great slab of mountain oak hung with forged hardware nothing short of dynamite could have forced from without. The rest of the sheriff's office was similarly constructed. It was, some said, the oldest log building in Gunsight. Old Jacob said it had originally been built by trappers as a fort, and many times Mulaney had reason to outspokenly condemn the short-sightedness of its builders because, with its two-foot thick sod roof and windowless, massive log walls, it was a veritable oven during the hot months.

Even when Mulaney had no reason to fret during Wyoming's summers, his granite character was not leavened any by soaring temperatures within his combination office and jail. But now, with a prisoner on his hands and an uneasy feeling in his mind, Sheriff Mike's irascibility was just barely below the boiling point.

"Mister," he said forcefully to Pete Knight through the cell bars, "I don't expect you to say you're a gunfighter . . . but do us both a favor and don't say anything at all for a while. I'm sick up to here of just listening to you."

Behind the bars young Knight, with both hands curled around the steel bars, knuckles white from holding, watched Mulaney go to his desk, fling down his hat, and mop sweat off his face. "I gave you everything you need to find out about me," he stated forcefully, ignoring Mulaney's request for silence. "Why don't you send telegrams and . . ."

"The nearest telegraph station is sixty miles from here," broke in Mulaney, glaring. "How many times I got to tell you that?"

"You can send someone. Wire my brother . . . he'll . . ."

"I don't want to hear about your damned brother anymore."

Mulaney flung himself down at the desk. Behind him, the prisoner considered his back a moment, then spoke again, his voice sharply edged with frustration and indignation.

"You got no right to hold me here. You got to let me out sooner or later. When are you going to get it through your head I'm no gunfighter. If one is coming here . . . I can't help that. But I swear to you . . . like I already said a dozen times . . . I'm only . . ."

"Yeah, I know. You're just a rider looking for work. You've heard Diamond H is a good paying outfit." Mulaney pushed back, arose, crushed on his hat, and stalked toward the door. "Knight, I got no idea how good you are with a gun, but I'll tell you one thing . . . if you aren't good enough to gun down the men you go after, you can always talk 'em to death."

Mulaney passed out of the office, carefully locked the door after himself, then went mutteringly along the plank walk toward the Drovers' and Cattlemen's Restaurant. Around him, evening shadows were beginning to puddle out in the roadway, to lengthen across the store fronts, and darken the valley sides or the mountains. As he passed those idlers' benches under the cottonwood tree he was relieved to see they were empty. Everyone, but particularly Gunsight's idlers, knew better how a sheriff should work than the sheriff did himself. He

23

rarely passed the tree that someone didn't volunteer an opinion on what he was doing wrong, and how he should operate. He turned into the restaurant, stalked up to the log counter, and dropped down on one of the stools.

"Supper for me," he said to the fat man behind the counter, "and a tray for my prisoner."

The fat man nodded stoically but did not offer to move toward the kitchen with any hurry. Instead, he leaned a little, lowering his voice as he did so, and spoke. "Mike, there's a lot of feeling around. In here I get the tag ends of a lot of conversations. I thought I ought to warn you about . . ."

Mulaney raised his bitter gaze and halted the fat man's speech in mid-sentence with it. "Just the supper," he said tonelessly. "Just the damned food, Buck."

Later, eating his own meal, Sheriff Mulaney reflected: his prisoner had none of the hardness, the assurance, or the attitude, of a gunman. This bothered him. But on the other hand, you could never know about gunmen. They didn't advertise. They tried not to appear as they really were. Consequently, short of finding their faces upon Wanted dodgers, you could never be certain.

Mulaney had looked through every dodger he'd ever received. His prisoner's face was not among them. He had read descriptions until his eyes ached, too, and again there had been nothing.

He drank two cups of coffee and made a cigarette, scowling into his cup. He had never been a man to put stock in rumors, but neither had he been a man who took chances when it was unnecessary to do so. Thus, in the end he had heeded rumor this time, believing it wiser to jail this stranger to his town first, in that way avoiding trouble, until he could ascertain exactly who his prisoner was.

Gunsight was, he knew, seething with anger at Diamond H. Arthur Hobart, the valley's biggest cattleman, had never, since Mulaney could remember, treated the town as anything but an essential evil. He had supported his riders' indiscretions in the town and had finally, only two weeks earlier, hurled the threat which Gunsighters were now practically up in arms about. He had said openly in the Cross Timbers Saloon that if the townsmen didn't stop victimizing his riders, he'd burn Gunsight to the ground. Then, when he was challenged about this by several local Gunsighters who were present when he made this statement, he had rallied his riders, stared down the townsmen, and, before stalking out, made one last remark. He would, he said, bring in his own law enforcer, and when he did that the townsmen had better walk softly.

Now, mused Mulaney, he had a man in his jail who, rumor was convinced, was this law enforcer.

The trouble was, thought Mulaney, he had an intuitive feeling he had the wrong man in jail. On the other hand, no strangers had appeared in Gunsight since Hobart had made that statement. Mulaney got up, tossed down some coins, took the prepared tray for his prisoner's supper, and left the restaurant. There was probably only one way to find out whether Pete Knight was Hobart's enforcer or not. It was to do exactly as Knight himself had requested—send someone down to the telegraph station at Casper.

CHAPTER THREE

Sheriff Mike Mulaney let himself into the office of the jailhouse, barred the door from the inside, and took Knight's supper across to him. As he slid the tray under the cell door, he said: "I'm going to send a man over to Casper to send those telegrams about you." As he straightened up, he added: "I hope that satisfies you."

Knight's boyish gray gaze slightly brightened, then it turned ironic. He wagged his head at Mulaney. "Sure takes a long time for something to get through your skull." He took up the tray, passed farther back to the bunk of his cell, and perched there to eat.

Mulaney watched a moment, then sighed and went to his desk.

The hours ticked by slowly. Mulaney, having thought it best to stay with the prisoner for the night, eased himself back down into his chair after having walked around the office to take the kinks out of his back and legs. No sooner had he settled when there was a hard rap at the door, which brought him fully upright again.

"Mike?" a voice called. "It's Slim. I want to see you a minute."

Mulaney crossed to the door, raised the bar, and pulled. The door swung inward. Five masked

27

men instantly sprang inside. Mulaney, taken totally by surprise, looked blankly from their shrouded faces to their bared pistols. Slowly a ruddy flush darkened his face.

"What do you think you're doing?" he demanded, still holding to the door. "Take those silly flour sacks off, put up those guns, and get out of here."

"Mike, we're going to take this here killer off your hands. Now you just rest easy-like and it'll all be over with in . . ."

"Slim, of all the dumb stunts you ever pulled in a lifetime full of dumb stunts, this is the dumbest. Now get out of here before I lock the lot of you up and throw away the key!"

The tallest of the masked men stared hard at Sheriff Mulaney before he cocked his six-gun. This sharp, mechanical sound froze everyone in the office, even Pete Knight, who was standing like stone staring at the intruders from inside his cell.

The masked man Sheriff Mulaney had addressed as Slim, now said: "Mike, you got no call to use that tone of voice to us. We're doing you a favor, taking this Diamond H gunfighter off your hands."

"Diamond H nothing," Mulaney stormed, entirely angry now, the astonishment and shock passed. "There's no proof yet who this fellow is. And you know that as well as I do."

"Proof enough for us," a masked man snarled. He flagged at Mulaney with his six-gun. "Go over by the desk and shut up." To the others around him, this man said: "One of you fellows get the key. Slim, keep watch at the door." Whoever this man was, he spoke and acted as though he had done this before. "Go on now," he said to Sheriff Mulaney, who had not moved from the door. "Over by your desk."

After a tense half minute, his hands balling into tight fists, Mulaney finally obeyed, his lips drawn flat and his eyes venomous.

As a masked man took up his key ring, Sheriff Mulaney said to him: "You touch that prisoner and so help me I'll see you in prison for it. Put those keys down!"

The masked man, flinching from Mulaney's tone and murderous stare, hesitated. The man over by the door whose narrow face showed its definite thin angularity even under the flour-sack mask, cried sharply: "Toss me them keys!"

This was done. The narrow-faced man started forward.

In the cell Pete Knight shrank back against the farthest wall. From behind the narrow-faced man, who had holstered his six-gun to work the lock and key, Mulaney said: "I know every one of you. You touch my prisoner and I'll see every man jack of you in hell! Get away from that door!"

The man over by the door flung down the keys, pulled open the door, then turned about to look steadily at Mulaney. He was obviously having troubled thoughts and said now: "Listen, we're telling you again . . . we're doing you a favor. You know Hobart will get some Cheyenne lawyers and get this fellow turned loose."

Mulaney swore at this man, then exclaimed sharply: "Whatever give you the idea I'd let you have a prisoner of mine . . . this man or anyone else? He's going to have a hearing and I'm going to be . . ."

"Mulaney! You're a fool. You'd better go along. The whole town favors this and you know it."

"The whole town be damned!" cried Sheriff Mike Mulaney. "I'm sheriff here. I know my job, and I sure as hell aim to do it. I'm going to tell you fellows just once more . . . get out of here!"

All but the masked man by the cell winced under Mulaney's vehement attack. Two of them looked at their associate near to Pete Knight's cage. The others continued to watch Sheriff Mulaney's mottled face swollen with rage.

The man by the cell turned his back upon the sheriff, glared at Pete Knight, and, without speaking, gestured for the prisoner to pass out of the cell.

Knight did not at once obey. His face turned a pale gray, rooted and unbelieving.

"Listen, you fellows," he began to say. "I swear

to you I'm no gunfighter. I came here because I heard the pay was good at the Diamond H Ranch. That's all. I never . . ."

"Out! Move out of there!" came the order.

Knight looked past at Mulaney. He stared at the other men in the office, then he pushed off the back wall and passed out of the cell. He stopped and half twisted, as though to make another appeal to the masked man behind him.

At that moment the masked man by the cell said bleakly to Mulaney: "Get in this cell."

"You go to hell," snarled the sheriff.

There was an abrupt change in the atmosphere. Beyond Mulaney's office darkest night dripped its formlessness over Gunsight. It was a little past midnight. The town was dark and silent.

"Mulaney, I'm telling you for the last time . . . get in that cell!"

No one moved. The sheriff's fire-pointed glare did not waver. "Hogan," he said, each word falling into the hush like flakes of iron. "You lynch this fellow and you'll die for it." Mulaney looked slowly around at the other masked men. Names fell from his lips in the identical merciless tone. "Slim Evans, Colt Balfrey, Will Holt, Bob Hogan. You think those masks will protect you? They won't. Not by a damned sight. I know every cussed one of you." He glared even though he couldn't see their faces. "You too, Frank. Frank Bell."

31

Knight, from the corner of his eye, saw the narrow-faced man's bared six-gun tip upward slightly and grow steady on the sheriff.

The narrow-faced man said swiftly: "Sheriff, shut up and do like he told you. Get in the cell!"

Mulaney did not respond but he slowly swung his hot gaze upon the prisoner. He seemed to weigh something briefly in his mind, then he inclined his head slightly. "I'm sorry, kid. You're no gunfighter. I'm sorry it had to come out like this. I reckon it's my fault."

"Go on," the young cowboy said, past dry lips. "Do like they want. Let them lock you up."

Mulaney stood without moving only a second longer, then he slumped. "Sure," he said, starting forward past his desk, past Pete Knight, and nearly past the masked man with the steadied gun. There, he went flat on his heels and hurled himself forward with a cry. It was a foolish and fatal and heroic thing to do.

Mulaney's straining body was against Hogan. They staggered together until brought up against the cell front. There, muffled by Mulaney's body, the masked man's revolver discharged. It was a meaty, tearing sound. Mulaney, knocked backward by force and impact, stared unbelievingly at the man who had shot him. He went forward from the middle, spilling out his full length upon the floor. He did not move again.

One of the masked men made a sharp, animal cry in his throat and flung around in the direction of the door.

Hogan's voice lashed out at this man. "He knew us. There wasn't no other way."

One of the others, equally as frightened, said: "Let's go, Hogan. Folks more than likely heard that shot."

"Take the prisoner," replied Hogan swiftly, moving away from Sheriff Mulaney's body. "Hurry up now. Down to the tree."

Pete Knight had not moved. He was staring down at Sherriff Mike Mulaney as a dark stain blossomed out from the bullet hole and stained his shirt and the floor around him.

Hogan came up and slammed his gun barrel into Knight's back causing sharp anguish.

"Move, damn you!" he shouted.

Knight moved. He shuffled forward like a sleepwalker. Beyond the sheriff's office in the pit of the night he revived, drew erectly upright and paused. One of the lynchers had produced a coiled lariat from inside his shirt. One end of it had been carefully fashioned into a hangman's knot.

"Straight ahead," the man beside Knight muttered. "Straight up to that big cottonwood yonder." He emphasized his command with a rough shove.

Knight passed along. He offered no resistance

until they laid hands upon him, turned him half about, and pushed and pulled until he was directly beneath a great shaggy lower limb.

Then he said to them what a calm man considers in the face of death. "I wouldn't want what you're doing on my conscience. I can prove I'm no gunfighter. But even if I was, fellows, I haven't broken any laws in your town."

A man expertly tossed the lariat over that burly limb. He worked grimly with the rope, never once looking at the others clustered there in the night.

The broken breathing of all of them lingered, loud in the hush of past midnight. Around them, Gunsight slept soundly. Not even a prowling alley cat saw what was going forward beneath Gunsight's solitary big cottonwood tree. Store fronts, their squared windows of black glass reflecting the sullenness of a nearly moonless night, stared out where six men clustered. None speaking for a time. None looking at one another until the rope was in place.

"Gunfighter," Hogan said finally, his voice barely loud enough to be heard, "you got half a minute to make a prayer."

Knight stood like stone, sweat standing out upon his forehead, his upper lip. The hard-twisted rope was in place, its big knot lying casually across one shoulder.

"I've *been* praying," he told them, his tone both

hollow sounding and slightly hoarse. "Hobart didn't send for me. I swear to you that's the truth. Why can't you wait another day . . . just one more day . . . and I'll pay one of you to ride to Casper and send telegrams to prove I'm not what you think I am."

It was a desperate and a futile plea. If Knight had reflected a moment, he would have known it was. They had murdered Mike Mulaney. The only witness besides those implicated was their prisoner. He had to die. If not for being what they believed him to be, then because he could name each of them. He had heard Mulaney identify each one.

Hogan jerked his head. "Fetch one of them benches," he ordered. Then he did not lower his eyes from Knight's face until the bench was brought forth and put carefully into place. He then said to Knight: "Step up onto that bench."

Knight looked around and down. Sweat glistened upon his face now.

"Come on," Hogan said impatiently. "Get up there."

They seized his bound arms and legs. They strained to raise him up onto the bench. Someone drew up all the rope's slack. The knot was snugged beneath Knight's right ear.

Knight made a desperate plea.

They did not let him finish it.

"Pull," said Hogan. "Make it fast around the

35

tree." He indicated the rope with his pistol hand. "Now the bench."

He watched his companions make the rope fast, then Hogan raised his left leg, put the foot strongly upon the bench, drew in a breath, and kicked. The bench went out from under Knight.

One of the masked men turned to lean upon the tree trunk, but only for a second, then sprang away with a little whimper.

Pete Knight's fierce plungings and writhings reverberated, sending up faint rustlings among the leaves, and shudders downward into the great bole of Gunsight's big cottonwood tree.

Hogan passed around behind the hanging man, saying swiftly to the others: "Never mind watching him. Listen to me now. Not a word to anyone. Forget this night ever passed. You hear me? Don't even talk about it among yourselves. It *never* happened! Now go on home. Burn them masks, go to bed, and tomorrow act natural."

As one, they lowered their eyes gradually, as Knight's struggles diminished—as his relaxed and sack-like dark silhouette turned slowly, then turned slowly back again, half around and half back around.

They continued to gaze upon Bob Hogan saying nothing. Again, he repeated his instructions, enunciating very clearly. Then he holstered his pistol and inclined his head at them.

"Go on now. It had to be done. We did a good

lick tonight for Gunsight. Hobart will know now we aren't any bunch of lily livers. So go home now . . . and remember . . . not a word about this to anyone as long as you live."

They began moving away in different directions. They were almost immediately lost in night's darkness. They made no sound in their passing. Hogan, the last to leave, waited until he could no longer distinguish any of them, then he yanked off his mask to show a fiercely exulting expression when he turned for a final look at the dead man twisting gently behind him. Then he too hastened away.

It was the last time all five of the lynchers stood together on earth.

CHAPTER FOUR

The body of Pete Knight was first discovered by Calvin Taylor, the day man at the livery barn. Taylor arose hours before sunup every day, went down to the barn, and relieved the night man. Invariably he had to awaken the night hawk; invariably too, they afterward had a cup of coffee together before the night man departed to sleep away the day.

Taylor plodded along through the cool darkness of before dawn scarcely looking up at all. As usual, Gunsight was as still as death, the roadway was totally empty, and Cal Taylor's footfalls sounded hollowly loud upon the plank walk. He turned in at the barn, went to the harness room, found the night hawk asleep as usual, shook him gently, and then passed over to the little iron stove to heat the coffee.

The night man groaned a little, turned up on his side upon the harness room's only bunk, and resumed his snoring.

Taylor, finished at the stove, turned to look down.

"Hogan!" he called. "Come on. It's near daybreak."

The resting man did not move.

Taylor went across to him, grinning a little. He shook him again, harder this time.

"Hey, Bob. Time to go home. I put the coffee on."

The night hawk sat up, gouged at both eyes with fisted hands, yawned prodigiously, explored his inner mouth with his tongue, and spat aside. "Sleepin' like a baby," he told the day man.

"You sure was."

"The coffee ready?"

"Pretty soon. Anything new come in last night?"

"Naw," said Hogan. "Quiet as a church yard around here last night." He stood up, stretched from the waist, then shuffled over to the stove to peer into the coffee pot. "Not enough here for two cups," he said to Taylor. "Fetch some more water, will you?"

Taylor left the harness room. He caught up a small bucket and passed through the barn's wide front entrance. He halted where a hand pump of rusty iron stood at one end of the water trough that was out front. He hooked the bucket onto the pump's upper prong, lifted the handle high, and started down with it, at the same time shooting a complacent gaze down the roadway.

His breath caught up. The hand on the pump handle froze. He stood there slightly bent forward from the waist with his eyes popped wide and staring. "Hell," he breathed.

It was an eternity packed into ten seconds. Taylor let go the pump handle. Slowly he straightened up and turned stiffly to pass back into the barn. His face was the color of ashes.

"Bob? Hey, Bob?"

"Yeah?"

"Come out here."

Hogan appeared in the harness room doorway. He cast a long look at Taylor before saying: "What's wrong with you, Cal?"

"Come out here," muttered Taylor, turning about, flat-footedly retracing his steps.

When they were standing together by the pump, Taylor raised an arm, pointing. "Look yonder . . . hanging in the tree."

Hogan looked. He grimaced and was silent before he finally said with difficulty: "Go fetch the sheriff."

Then, as Calvin Taylor started forward, gradually increasing his pace until he was nearly running to Mike Mulaney's jail house office, Bob Hogan's lips drew back, and he threw a savage and mirthless smile at the hanging corpse of Pete Knight.

Gunsight learned in some mysterious manner, even before it was fully awake and stirring, that Mike Mulaney had been killed in his own office, and that his prisoner had been lynched.

It was as though a sigh of premonition, of

41

shame and guilt and fear, had come with the first morning breeze to settle upon the town.

Pete Knight was cut down and placed beside Sheriff Mike in the embalming shed behind Doc Parmenter's buggy shack. No one went to view either body, and because Doc Parmenter was out at one of the cow outfits where he'd spent the night awaiting the culmination of a cowman's wife's labor pains, he did not know until early afternoon when he returned to town what had happened.

It was Dr. Parmenter who found in the lynched cowboy's pocket a ragged old letter from a man whose signature was simply: **Ben Knight**. There was an address, indifferently scrawled, which Doc had trouble deciphering. But when he had it translated, he told no one. He simply wrote a formal letter of notification and regret, addressed it to U.S. Deputy Marshal Ben Knight, Denver, Colorado, and mailed it. Then, still keeping his counsel, Doc Parmenter prepared both bodies for burial and saw them put into the ground at Gunsight's cemetery, which was south of town a distance, encircled by a sturdy iron fence.

Doc Parmenter, an elderly man whose perpetually squinted, shrewd eyes had viewed a lot of living, then composed himself to wait. He had no family of his own and he made a habit of studying people, of gauging them. He had been both shocked and angered by the dual killings. He felt in his heart that if Hobart had bullied Gunsight, the townsmen in their way had brought much of it upon themselves. He had heard of Hobart's threat. But he also knew that Diamond H's antipathy toward Gunsighters was fully justified.

Days passed. Doc Parmenter went his rounds. He recognized the uneasiness of the townsmen. He even heard a few remarks that, if there might have been reason for lynching the man everyone still thought was a hired gunfighter, there was no reason at all for the killing of Mike Mulaney.

It was their sheriff's murder, more than the grisly sight which had greeted their startled eyes the morning after Knight's lynching, which contributed most to the townspeople's subdued grimness now. If, they told one another, whoever had shot Sheriff Mike like that—at such close range his clothing had caught fire and partially burned—had been so unreasoning and savage as to murder a man who they knew had committed no crime—was it not entirely possible that the young cowboy they had also murdered was likewise guiltless?

It took slightly less than a week for the people of Gunsight to come entirely down from their antagonism toward Arthur Hobart's Diamond H cow outfit and face this new situation. They had not bargained for anything like this. They had been angered by Hobart's threat and they would have met him openly with force if he had come into their town seeking trouble. But this—this wanton butchering of men, one of whom was known to be definitely their own friend, turned most of the people of Gunsight morose.

If they had known of Doc Parmenter's letter they might also have felt apprehensive. But only Parmenter knew of this, and he said nothing. He kept quiet for the best of reasons too. One quiet stranger had ridden into Gunsight wearing a gun and he had been hanged within thirty-six hours of his arriving there. Doc thought, if Ben Knight came at all, he deserved a better chance for survival. He deserved the chance to live, which had been denied his brother. Doc was not a vindictive man, but he had lived a long time on the frontier. He believed unreservedly in fair play. This time he meant to see that a stranger riding into Gunsight got it.

No one was appointed by Gunsight's town council to replace Sheriff Mike. Two local men were queried, but both declined. For the time being then, Gunsight was without a combination town marshal and county sheriff. The work piled up, the town councilmen did what of it they could—the paperwork anyway—and fortunately, in its depressed condition, Gunsight had no real trouble.

• • •

The second week after Mulaney's killing, Arthur Hobart appeared in Gunsight with his foreman, Ace Dwinell, and the Diamond H ranch wagon. They put in at the hitch rail before Blakely's Emporium, sought out Richard Blakely, and gave him their provisions list. Then, without speaking further with Blakely, Hobart and his foreman stalked to the northernmost extremity of Gunsight and entered the Cross Timbers Saloon.

The news of Hobart's arrival in town spread swiftly, as it always did, but this time no cliques formed upon the plank walk to mutter against the Diamond H, and Mike Mulaney did not come out of his office to stare down potential troublemakers.

Gunsight was aware of Hobart's grim presence, but it had something else on its mind—a general feeling of depression, of guilt and shame. It still did not like Diamond H and Arthur Hobart, but now it simply wanted him to quietly ride away. The townsmen had no stomach for fighting. Not right then.

Hobart and Dwinell did their silent drinking at the Cross Timbers, then went down to the Drovers' and Cattlemen's hash house and ate heartily, saying nothing to anyone. After eating they returned to Blakely's store, viewed the mounds of supplies heaped in their ranch wagon, and, instead of leaving town, entered the

Emporium. They walked directly up to Blakely, both smelling of Old Taylor and garlic, and halted.

"Blakely," said Arthur Hobart, his dark and hawk-like countenance solemn, "you still a town councilman?"

"Yes," the merchant responded, feeling uneasy.

"I got a message for you, then," said the cowman, his hard eyes glinting with pleasure. "Find the men who pulled the rope to hang that young cowboy and drive them north out of town by sundown tonight . . . or face the consequences."

Richard Blakely blanched. He was a thin and nervous man with a smile that came and went and meant nothing. Now he blinked, looked from Hobart to Dwinell, and made his inane smile.

"Listen, Mister Hobart," he said weakly. "That's past. We're all awful sorry about that. And about Mike, too, but it's past and you got no call to . . ."

"It's not me," Hobart said shortly. "This time it's not Diamond H, Blakely. I don't care what you do with those hang ropers. They're Gunsighters, so I don't personally give a damn what you do with 'em. You can shoot 'em or tar and feather 'em."

"Then . . . who, Mister Hobart?"

"A stranger who come down across the mountains on to my range about sunup this morning and rode into our foothill cow camp . . . *he* sent you that word."

"A stranger?"

"Yeah, a stranger," grunted Hobart. "His name isn't strange though . . . it's Knight. Ben Knight." Hobart's dully glistening stare sharpened.

Blakely went pale. He was staring at Hobart silently.

"I see you recollect the name, Blakely." Hobart turned on his heel. "Better pass that message along to the town council. The stranger said have 'em herded out of town by sundown."

Blakely called after the cowman in a weak tone. "Mister Hobart . . . ?"

"Yeah."

"Ask him to come here where we can explain about what happened."

Hobart shook his head. "Can't," he said. "He only come down to my cow camp to have someone fetch you townsmen that message. Then he went back into the mountains." Arthur Hobart paused. He smiled at the merchant, this time, because he was genuinely enjoying himself, and that amusement showed itself in Hobart's smile. "You bunch of fools," he said, around his grin. "I didn't even know that cowboy's name until after you'd hung him. I didn't send for him. I haven't sent for anyone . . . yet."

Hobart and Dwinell left the store.

Richard Blakely went to a counter and leaned there. He breathed shallowly. There was a constricting band squeezing his heart. With fumbling fingers, he removed his apron, placed it upon the counter, and beckoned forward a clerk.

"Mind the store," he told his employee. "I have got to see the other councilmen."

He left the store with uneven steps, paused just long enough to shoot a glance at the sun's overhead position, then he scuttled through roadway dust toward Jacob Howell's saddle shop.

He was with old Jacob only a few minutes, then he fled along the plank walk to the livery barn. There, he spoke swiftly to Gus Cawley, the owner, and afterward left Gus staring after him as he sped to the northernmost building in Gunsight, the Cross Timbers Saloon.

At the bar he fell into a chair to speak desperately to Morgan Hyatt, owner of the Cross Timbers. He had then carried Ben Knight's message to each member of Gunsight's Town Council.

The afternoon ran on. People went on about their business in their normal subdued way. For a while Gunsight seemed as usual. But then, very gradually, things changed.

Men stood upon the plank walk speaking together, gazing both ways along the roadway, and from time to time eyeing the huge orange disc hanging up there in the summer sky. Womenfolk completed their shopping and left the town empty of their presences. Only an occasional child appeared, and after a time—by two o'clock in the afternoon—they too had disappeared.

Gunsight waited. It was without sounds at all. At Blackwell's blacksmith shop the men sat in shade, some smoking, some simply gazing along the road. By three o'clock only a few very bold men were visible along the plank walks.

Gunsight was in appearance a ghost town.

CHAPTER FIVE

Doc Parmenter heard the soft roll of knuckles over his front door and moved leisurely in response. It had been a quiet day for the doctor; only a snake-bitten child and a cowboy from south of town with a purple and swollen foot where a horse had stepped on him, had taken up his time. He had also napped—something he did not often have an opportunity to do. So he felt mellow and genial as he opened the door and considered the tall, steady-eyed man who stood there with trail dust powdered upon his dark clothing. This stranger had a composed face. He seemed a thoughtful, reflective type man, Parmenter thought as he studied him. Then the big man spoke and Doc Parmenter's mellowness dissolved.

"I got your letter, Doctor," the stranger said. "I'm Ben Knight."

Parmenter's shaggy brows drew out across his face. His shrewd eyes dimmed a little. He stepped aside. "Come in, Mister Knight."

He closed the door after Ben Knight and motioned toward the chairs in his parlor. Without speaking, he took a chair himself and sank down.

Knight crossed to stand nearby but he did not sit down or remove his hat. He was considering Dr. Parmenter impassively.

Parmenter noted that there was something about Ben Knight that was not readily definable. He looked more than capable, but that wasn't it. He wore a gun like a man fully accustomed to not only wearing it, but also using it. But it wasn't this either. Or, to Parmenter's mind, at least this was not all of it.

After a bit more observation of Ben Knight, Dr. Parmenter, student of humanity, finally put his finger upon this elusive thing: Ben Knight was perfectly co-ordinated. He was entirely confident. He was . . . deadly.

"I won't bother you," Knight now said in that deep but soft voice Parmenter had noted at the door. "I just want some names, Doctor."

Parmenter sighed. He rummaged his pockets for his pipe. "I can't give them to you," he replied. "Even if I knew them, I don't think I'd give them to you." He found the pipe, loaded it, fired up, and stoked it with a thumb pad. Over the smoke he studied Ben Knight. "You think killing them will bring your brother back?"

"It'll make him rest easier, Doctor."

Parmenter wagged his head. "You don't believe that," he retorted. "The dead are dead." He gestured again toward a chair. "Sit down, young man. I don't like looking up at you."

Ben Knight did not move. Dr. Parmenter sighed resignedly and leaned back. "They killed our sheriff, too. I forgot to tell you that in the letter."

Parmenter puffed a moment, then said: "You're a lawman, Mister Knight. Would you help out here until a replacement can be found for our dead sheriff?"

Knight's gray gaze turned smoky. He made a little smile with his lips and shook his head. "You're pretty wise," he told the doctor. "No thanks. I'm not a lawman now. You can't bait me into putting on a badge, Doctor. I know what's in your mind." He paused for effect. "A local lawman couldn't hunt down those responsible for the murder of my brother . . . and kill them."

Parmenter peered into his pipe bowl, tamped it gingerly, and plugged it back into his mouth. "The boy rode into Gunsight," he recapitulated now. "They thought he was a hired gunfighter, and they took him out in the night and hung him."

"He was no gunfighter. He was just a kid."

"Yes, just a kid."

"Why didn't they try to find out who he was first?"

"Mister Knight, did you ever hear of a lynch mob that had any sense at all? Of course you haven't because if those men had had any sense, they never would have been there with your brother under the cottonwood tree."

"I know," murmured the tall man, who paused then to watch the older man's face before adding: "You travel around a lot, Doctor. You've heard names mentioned."

53

"Probably the wrong ones. Would you want them?"

"No."

"Mister Knight, no one knows who lynched your brother. No one in Gunsight knows I wrote you, either. I don't believe, the way folks feel now, they'd lynch another stranger, but I preferred not to tempt them."

Knight's brows drew slightly downward. "No one knows about me?" he asked.

Dr. Parmenter shook his head and puffed up a gray cloud. "Mike Mulaney may have known about you, but he's dead. As far as I know, there is not a soul in town who knows your brother had living kin. In all the talk that's going around, no one has mentioned this possibility around me."

Parmenter stopped and squinted his eyes at Knight. He removed his pipe and held the bowl cupped in one hand.

"It's up to you, my boy. You can ferret them out and kill them. I have an idea that's in your mind. Or you can do this thing the way it ought to be done."

"How is that?" the tall man asked, showing plainly by his expression that he knew what Parmenter's reply would be.

"Bring them to the bar of justice, Mister Knight. You're not God. It's not your job to judge them . . . to execute them."

Knight began to move across the room toward

the door. "I think it's my duty to execute them, Doctor, not my job." He lifted the latch, hesitated only a second, then passed out of the house.

Dr. Parmenter sucked at his pipe again. It had gone out, so he put it aside and looked at a large mantle clock.

"I know the kind," he told the clock, speaking aloud his thoughts after the manner of men much alone. "I've patched them up and I've buried them. The Jesse Jameses of this world . . . the Will Hickoks . . . the Daltons and Renos."

Parmenter arose, shook his head, and stalked over to a front window to peer out. "Within the law or beyond the law," he said, "they're killers." His gaze strayed along Gunsight's roadway where fading sunlight slanted, and very slowly it came to him that the roadway was unnaturally empty. He stopped speaking aloud and peered more sharply at the town. "Now what the hell . . . ?" he said grumpily, and crossed to a rack, took down his hat, and left the house.

As Dr. Parmenter passed beyond his front gate four horsemen riding slowly, scuffed down through the roadway dust. He squinted outward at them. One, the foremost rider, he recognized instantly—Arthur Hobart.

Parmenter increased his pace and turned in at Blakely's Emporium. He asked the clerk, who looked worried, the whereabouts of Blakely.

The clerk's expression of anxiety deepened.

"They're in the back room," he told Parmenter, "but they said they weren't to be disturbed."

"They?" the doctor asked testily. "Who is 'they'?"

"The town council."

Parmenter digested this thoughtfully, then turned to watch Hobart and his Diamond H horsemen plod past out where the lowering sun was reddening Gunsight. He thought Hobart's forbidding, sun-rusted countenance looked bleakly pleased. He could imagine with little difficulty what caused this pleasure. Hobart knew the hanged cowboy's gun-fighting brother had arrived in the valley. How he knew, Parmenter couldn't guess, but that did not trouble him right then. Hobart had come to town with his toughest riders. He obviously meant to linger in Gunsight in anticipation of trouble.

This started the doctor on a new train of thought. He faced back, considered the closed far door behind which Gunsight's administrators were in session, then he shrugged, saying to the clerk: "What's going on in town? It's as quiet as a graveyard out there. Not a soul in sight."

The clerk shot a look out the front window at the descending sun. "Haven't you heard?" he said. "That there cowboy that got lynched . . . his brother has shown up and he's in the hills north of town somewhere. He sent word to the councilmen to drive the fellows who lynched

56

that cowboy beyond town before sundown . . . or else." A shiver seemed to run down the clerk's back.

Dr. Parmenter's seamed old face very gradually creased with deep perplexity. "In the mountains, you say? No . . . he can't be up there."

"Oh, yes he can," retorted the clerk warmly. "Hobart's men saw him this morning. He sent the message in by Hobart himself."

Dr. Parmenter pinched his lips with the fingers of one hand, staring at the floor, then, a moment later, he left Blakely's Emporium bound for the livery barn. There, he talked for a while with Calvin Taylor before heading for Jacob Howell's saddlery, where he drew out a chair behind the front window, leaned far back in it so the front legs were off the floor, and cocked his booted feet upon Jacob's display shelf. In this fashion he sat motionlessly for the length of time it took for old Jacob to return from the council meeting. By that time, too, Dr. Parmenter had smoothed out and carefully arranged his thoughts.

What he had deduced did not please him, either. Jacob, entering his shop, saw Parmenter's grim expression, tossed aside his flat-brimmed hat, scratched his mane of white hair, and began belting his working apron around him, as he said: "Going to be some killings, Doc. I reckon you heard, though."

Parmenter did not immediately reply.

57

"We got to get a marshal for town right quick, too," went on the old saddle maker. "Just had a meeting over at Blakely's about that . . . and this Knight fellow."

"Which Knight fellow?" Parmenter growled, without looking away from the roadway.

"Why, the one's up in the hills loaded for bear."

"He's not up in the mountains, Jacob."

"What?"

"I said he's not up in the mountains," Parmenter repeated, and turned. They were both old men, nearly of an age. "What's the matter with you anyway, Jacob? You going deaf?"

Old Howell was stung. His faded blue eyes flashed. "Deaf like a wolf," he said sharply. "I could hear a Sioux draw his fleshing knife at a hundred yards."

"Hasn't been a hostile Indian around here in twenty years," Parmenter reminded the old shop-keeper. "Besides, a bronco buck couldn't even walk in the shadow of this here Ben Knight."

Jacob finished adjusting and tying on his apron. He stood a moment before his large work table considering an unrolled oak-tanned cowhide there. Then he turned slowly and threw a stare at Parmenter's back.

"Just how do you know about Ben Knight?" he demanded.

"Because, dammit, he was at my house not more than half an hour ago."

"At your house?"

"In my parlor."

Jacob Howell shuffled forward so he could peer into Parmenter's face. "You're joshing me," he said, but without any conviction in his voice. "You sure he was this Knight fellow?"

"I'm sure."

"How do you know you're sure?"

"I got eyes, Jacob," Doc Parmenter said, getting a bit annoyed.

Howell drew up his apron and sat down upon the edge of his display shelf near Dr. Parmenter's feet. He squinted. "You got to be wrong, Doc. A fellow can't be two places at once."

"I'm not wrong, Jacob." Parmenter brought the front legs of the chair down with a crash, gathered his legs under him, and arose. "It was Ben Knight all right. Even if he hadn't told me who he was, I'd have known. Don't forget I embalmed his brother. I caught the resemblance all right. He was Ben Knight!"

Jacob grew thoughtful. After a moment's reflection he said: "Something's wrong here, Doc. Hobart told Blakely that this here brother of Pete Knight come to his cow camp, give him a message for us townsfolk, then rode back into the mountains."

Parmenter's old face smoothed out a little. His eyes shone with hard irony. "Something's wrong all right," he said. "And I've been sitting here trying to figure it out."

"I'm listening," said old Jacob. "Go on."

"Keep this between us, Jacob. For the time being anyway. You understand?"

"You got my word, Doc. Shoot."

"Diamond H met Ben Knight somewhere. That part's true enough, and maybe Knight said why he was here . . . which is to kill the men who lynched his brother." Parmenter paused to rub his chin before continuing. "But the rest of it . . . that story about Knight demanding us to deliver the lynchers to him beyond town before sundown . . . that's Hobart's work. Don't ask me why Hobart's doing this. I can only guess about that . . . but he made up that message. Ben Knight never sent it."

"Did he tell you he didn't?"

"Of course not. How could he mention a message he didn't send? Trust me, he didn't mention it and neither did I. The reason I didn't was because I didn't know anything about it when he came to see me. The reason he didn't . . . I think . . . was because he didn't know anything about it either." Parmenter gazed downward at Howell.

The old saddle-maker was perplexed now. He sighed and wagged his head.

Parmenter then explained further. "A man who has thrown down a challenge to a town doesn't come riding into it in broad daylight, Jacob. Nor does he tie up at my front gate and pay me a social call."

"Doesn't seem likely he would," agreed Howell.

"Of course, he wouldn't. He'd know the whole town would be watching for him . . . that they'd throw down on him the minute he showed his face."

"Be pretty risky all right, Doc." Jacob Howell was briefly silent, then fixed Parmenter with a shrewd look. "Does this Knight fellow look like a damned fool?"

Parmenter snorted. "He's a long way from being that, Jacob. This fellow is a top-notch gunfighter. It's stamped all over him. He's maybe thirty years old, too. Gunmen don't get that old by being foolish, Jacob."

"No."

"And furthermore, he's after his brother's killers and he's going to find them, too. I wouldn't want to be in their boots, believe me."

Old Jacob got to his feet. He turned toward the window. "Like a ghost town out there," he murmured. "What you reckon is going to happen, Doc?"

"The Lord only knows, Jacob. Whatever Hobart's up to spells trouble. But Ben Knight is definitely somewhere around here. And believe you me, he's maybe even bigger trouble."

"We got to get that temporary lawman," Jacob said adamantly. "That's all there is to it."

Dr. Parmenter, also gazing out where dying day mantled Gunsight's broad and deserted roadway, made his derisive snort for the second time.

"Fat lot of good some amateur lawman's going to do now, Jacob. What Gunsight needs is a divine miracle."

Jacob turned away from the window. "Kathy was going to fetch supper down here to me," he told Parmenter. "Expect I'd better go home and tell her to stay off the walks until this here thing blows over."

"Good idea," muttered the medical man, moving toward the street-side door. He stopped there to fix a puzzled look upon Howell. "Hobart's timed this to coincide with Knight's arrival in Gunsight."

"It looks that way, doesn't it?"

"You got any idea why, Jacob?"

"No, I got no idea."

"Because, whatever he's got planned, will need a man to be blamed for it. Knight's supposed to be that man."

Old Jacob considered this, then shook his head as he said in a tired tone: "Dammit all, Doc . . . why'd those idiots go and lynch that young fellow, anyway?"

"I think," retorted Doc Parmenter with a grim expression on his face, "that a conscience is a pretty worthless thing, Jacob. It should bother folks *before,* not after, they think up meanness."

CHAPTER SIX

It appeared to those watching, that the sun descended with inordinate swiftness this day. By midafternoon everyone knew about Ben Knight's alleged message. They had also heard that Arthur Hobart and several of his riders were at the Cross Timbers Saloon. At Blakely's Emporium men passed inward, tarried long enough to speak with the harassed proprietor, then passed out again to spread what Blakely had told them in answer to their questions, among the other people of Gunsight.

Across the road at the livery barn Gus Cawley sweated bullets. He was a man who worried. If he wished for rain, and it came, Gus fretted for fear it would turn into a flood. He told the day man, Calvin Taylor, he thought Ben Knight might get the wrong names and shoot innocent men.

Taylor, not ordinarily a worrier, recalled without effort the vivid first view he'd had that morning when he'd discovered the hanged man. Up until Knight's appearance in the Gunsight country, Taylor had only been grimly bitter. Now he secretly hoped Knight might find those hang ropers. For some reason or other he did not believe Ben Knight would get the wrong men, but he said nothing of this to Gus.

In fact, all he did say was: "Folks sure changed the last couple weeks. First, they were all fired-up to catch Hobart's gunfighter. Then, after they hung that cowboy, all the fight oozed out of 'em."

"It's the injustice," replied Cawley, wincing from the recollection that he had been one of those whose outspoken and militant denunciation of Hobart had kept tempers white-hot. "It's one thing to lynch an outlaw and it's another thing to up and lynch an innocent man."

"Any proof yet that he was innocent, Gus? What I mean is . . . everyone's so busy being contrite, and all . . ."

Kathy Howell, old Jacob's granddaughter passed along the plank walk in full view and Cal's voice dwindled. She was the loveliest female in Gunsight, bar none.

Cal's eyes followed her admiringly.

"There's proof," said Cawley, scarcely sparing a glance for the beautiful blonde girl. "Hobart himself told Blakely he hadn't hired Knight."

Cal ambled to the threshold of the street-side door and leaned there, still watching Kathy Howell. She went as far as her grandfather's saddle shop and there she turned in. For a moment, slanting sunlight burnished the spun-like gold of her hair as she paused to turn a slow, penetrating glance upon the roadway's emptiness. Two small parallel lines appeared between her eyes. Then her grandfather's voice came forward to draw her attention.

"Don't stand there," commanded old Jacob from within the shop. "Come in, come in."

Kathy went as far forward as the work bench where Jacob was laying out a pattern for the leather seat, his faded eyes bright with concentration. There, she put a small basket upon the bench, saying: "Hello, Grandfather." Then she looked outside again, and added: "Why is everything so quiet today?"

Jacob sighed. He pulled his attention from the layout with an effort. He gazed long upon his lovely granddaughter before answering her. "Trouble over that young fellow someone lynched," he said.

"Trouble? What kind of trouble?" Worry washed across her face.

"He had a brother . . . a gunfighter, from what I been told. His brother's out there somewhere," Jacob indicated *out there* with a vague arm wave. "He's got his neck all bowed and there's blood in his eye."

"Hasn't anyone tried to stop him?"

Jacob blinked. "How?" he asked simply.

"Well," the girl said matter-of-factly, "get up a posse, go out and get him."

Jacob pursed his lips and nodded his head as he reached for the basket Kathy had brought him, peered under the checkered napkin, took out a crockery bowl and a spoon, and put them carefully down.

Then he said: "Honey, it isn't likely for a woman to think like a man. Particularly a real pretty woman." He smiled indulgently at his granddaughter and returned to rummaging the basket.

"What has that to do with it?" Kathy demanded.

Still indulgently, old Jacob said: "A posse rides out, like you suggest, and this lobo wolf up in the foothills watches it ride out. Then *he* rides down here."

"Leave men to guard the town."

Jacob's patience was getting a little thin. "That wouldn't do any good, honey. This man's a loner. You can run yourself ragged hunting his kind . . . but you never find 'em unless they want you to."

"So you're just going to sit here and let him . . ."

"Kathy!"

A dark shape loomed in the doorway. Jacob's eyes were upon the stranger. Kathy turned, too, also looking. Neither of them knew this man, who was obviously a range rider. He moved with the easy grace of a fully poised person. He nodded to them both but said nothing until he was close to the work bench, then, in deference to Kathy, he removed his hat. When he struck it against his leg, dust flew outward, gray and fine like powder.

"I'd like a little information," the tall stranger said, his voice softly deep and compelling. Then he paused, for old Jacob's seamed face had gone shades paler than usual.

"What kind of information, stranger?"

The tall man smiled disarmingly. At his hip rode a six-gun that was lashed down and whose original bluing had long since been worn away. The gun, however, had a handsomely carved walnut handle, and it showed care.

"I'd like to know where I might find a man named Arthur Hobart."

"Hobart?" Jacob said dumbly, staring at this big man's rugged countenance.

"Yes, Hobart."

A faint frown mantled the stranger's features. He returned Jacob's scrutiny with something close to puzzlement in his eyes.

"Well . . . I just don't rightly know," Jacob said hesitantly, his voice fading. "Maybe out at his ranch . . ."

"He's here in Gunsight," the tall man corrected the old saddle maker. "What I want to know is where he usually hangs out when he comes to town."

"You're sure he's here in town?"

"Plumb sure," replied the stranger. Then, fully frowning now, he said, in an altered, roughened tone: "What's bothering you, old-timer . . . did I say something I shouldn't have?"

"No," answered up Jacob swiftly. "No, you didn't say anything wrong."

Now Kathy spoke, diverting the stranger's attention from her grandfather.

"Mister Hobart and his riders usually spend their time here in town at the Cross Timbers Saloon. It's the last building at the north end of town."

"Thank you, ma'am," the tall man said, his gaze softening toward her. He hesitated the smallest part of a minute before beginning to turn away.

Kathy took advantage of his visible admiration to ask a question.

"What is your name?"

Old Jacob stiffened, not so much because he thought he already knew the answer and it frightened him, but because Kathy knew better than to ask strangers personal questions.

"Ben Knight," said the stranger, his eyes turning soft again as they lingered on her. Then he smiled, which made his otherwise impassive face quite handsome. "What's yours, ma'am?"

Kathy flushed, and yet, because she had challenged him, and he therefore had the right to do the same to her, she said: "Katherine Howell." Then, to divert his gaze, she added: "This is my grandfather, Jacob Howell."

Knight nodded at Jacob, who nodded back. He returned his smoky gaze to the girl, saying: "Thank you again." He began, for the second time, to head for the door, and again Kathy stopped him with words.

"Mister Knight, aren't you aware the people of Gunsight know who you are and why you're here?"

The gray gaze hardened just the slightest bit toward Jacob's lovely granddaughter as Ben Knight turned fully around to face her. "I reckon by now they do," he said. "Is there anything wrong in that, Miss Howell?"

Kathy hung fire just a second over her reply. When next she spoke, the conviction in her voice was less than before. "Well, but those men should be brought to trial . . . not just shot down for revenge."

Knight looked thoughtfully downward into Kathy's violet eyes. He appeared to be very solemn now. "Who is going to bring them in, ma'am? They tell me you've got no law here now . . . that the same men who lynched my brother murdered your sheriff."

"But, Mister Knight, that doesn't mean we can't get law here. And it doesn't mean you can just go find these men and shoot them down."

Again, Knight's answer was moments coming. He made a small smile at her, before saying: "So far, I'm not having too much luck even finding them. I figured maybe this Arthur Hobart might help me there."

For the first time Jacob Howell spoke up. "Not

Hobart," he told Knight. "He hates this town. He said he'd burn it to the ground. It was because of his saying he was going to send for a gunfighter to come here and take Gunsight over, that folks hung your brother, Mister Knight. The lad was the only stranger to ride in after Hobart said that." Jacob leaned upon the work bench. "If you go to Hobart, folks will naturally think you're on his side against the town, and it'll likely start the feuding all over again. Besides that, Hobart will tell you any names he wants to. But I don't think he knows any more about the murderers of your brother than anyone else does."

Jacob stopped talking and drew in a big breath. He fixed Knight with a supplicating stare and concluded with: "Right now you aren't going to get much sense out of anyone hereabouts, especially not after sending that message to the town council. Folks are too upset."

Ben Knight looked away from Kathy. He stared into Jacob's face.

"What message?" Knight asked.

Jacob's shoulders slumped. He returned the tall man's look over an interval of thoughtful silence, then he softly said: "I'll be damned. Doc Parmenter was right."

"Grandfather . . . ?" Kathy said, confused by the odd look on her grandfather's face.

"Quiet, Kathy," Jacob said in an uncommonly dismissive way. He remained thoughtful for a number of minutes, and then he said to Ben Knight: "Hobart come to town this morning, saying you'd sent word for Gunsight to find your brother's murderers and drive 'em out of town by sunset . . . or else."

Knight's dark brows drew inward and downward. "Go on," he quietly said. "What's the rest of it?"

Jacob made a gesture with his hands. "The town's waiting. It's just doing nothing but nervously watching the sun go down." Jacob's hands fell back to the work bench and remained there. "About two hours ago, Hobart and some of his Diamond H riders come to town. They're down at the Cross Timbers Saloon. They're just waiting like everybody else."

Ben Knight moved over to the work bench and leaned there, saying nothing, just staring at old Jacob. After a while he took his tobacco sack from a shirt pocket and deliberately twisted up a cigarette. Both Jacob and Kathy watched him light up, inhale, exhale, then twist to throw a reflective look outward through the front window to the empty roadway beyond.

When Kathy could scarcely tolerate the stillness any longer, Ben Knight faced back around looking straight into Jacob's eyes.

"I met some Diamond H riders this morning near the foothills. I asked a few questions, figuring they might know something about my brother's murderers. I sent no message to Gunsight by them or anyone else."

Jacob related what Doc Parmenter had told him earlier. To this Ben Knight replied musingly that he thought Parmenter must be right, that Hobart planned something for which he would need a victim. Then Knight drew up off the work bench and smiled at Jacob. It was not a pleasant smile at all.

"I guess I have to go and see this Hobart after all," he said. "Only now for a different reason." He swung around, looked squarely into Kathy's face, but, still speaking to Jacob, asked: "Who bought the last lariat you sold in here?"

Jacob, behind the tall man's back, gave a start. "Colt Balfrey," he answered, scarcely speaking loud enough to be heard.

"Thanks," said Knight, and then he left the saddle shop.

"Grandfather . . . ?"

"Not right now, honey," Jacob said distractedly. "You'd better drink some of the coffee I brought," Kathy advised.

Then she busied herself at the work bench. When she had the cup of coffee prepared, she lifted it and tried to hand it to him.

Old Jacob was looking through the window and out into the shadowed roadway.

"You know what I just done, Kathy?" he asked.

"No. Here . . . drink this while it's hot."

72

"I just killed a man."

Kathy's eyes sprang wide. She gently lowered the cup, set it aside, saying as she did so: "What do you mean?"

"I just killed a man, honey." Jacob turned slowly to meet her gaze. "He asked who bought the last lariat in here. Don't you see?"

"No, I don't see."

"His brother was hung with a lariat. The man who owned it bought a replacement."

"Oh," Kathy said a little above a whisper, her lips making an oval, the sound of this expression itself a sort of soft sigh. She understood.

"Why didn't I figure that out, too?" asked old Jacob.

He got no answer.

Kathy crossed to the doorway and stood there looking northward into the late afternoon.

CHAPTER SEVEN

Across the road and striding north toward the Cross Timbers Saloon was Ben Knight. He was the only visible person the length of Gunsight's main street. He walked with that unique confidence that set him apart from other men. Even knowing, as he did, that a dozen or more eyes were discreetly observing his passing, he strode along easily, glancing neither right nor left.

At Blakely's Emporium he sighted a white and startled face standing back from the entrance. Then he was past, the face was gone, and ahead loomed a listing old picket fence that had once been whitewashed, but which now was the color of bleached bones. Here, he also thought a pair of grave eyes might be watching, and he was correct. Doc Parmenter, hidden by the curtains of his parlor, his pipe cold between his lips and his hands clasped behind him, was staring out. He too saw Ben Knight go past.

The Cross Timbers Saloon was an older log building. Not as old as Jacob's saddle shop, but still older than most of Gunsight's buildings. Morgan Hyatt, who had founded the Cross Timbers, was a Texan. He had come north with a trail herd some sixteen years earlier, and he had stayed. In those former times he had been a lean-

75

hipped, heavy-armed, and burly-shouldered man. But sixteen years without appreciable exercise had given his once powerful body a noticeable sag and bulge. Still, Morgan Hyatt was a man to reckon with. It was said in the Gunsight country there was no man who could pin his shoulders to the floor in a free-for-all.

Another thing about Morgan—he had been born, weaned, and matured in the cowman's world. Although he was himself a confirmed townsman, he did not consider himself one. In the feud between Diamond H and the town, he had sympathized with Diamond H. And it was for this reason that Arthur Hobart patronized the Cross Timbers, and of course, since Hobart did this, so also did his riders.

It was Morgan, leaning upon the bar now, his paunch pressing strongly forward as he spoke with Arthur Hobart, who, glancing over the cowman's shoulder, saw the tall stranger push in out of the slanting afternoon sunlight and pace evenly forward toward the bar. Like Jacob Howell, Morgan Hyatt had an icy premonition. He drew gradually up off the bar, his countenance going cautious.

"Help you?" he inquired of the stranger.

Ben Knight made no reply. He looked from Arthur Hobart to the riders ranged along the bar beside him. One of these men he recognized as being a member of the cow-camp crew he'd spoken with earlier in the day. He addressed himself to this man, but there was no doubt as to whom he was actually speaking.

"When we met this morning," Knight said to the cowboy without preliminaries, "I asked you a few questions about a lynching. Is that right?"

"That's right," agreed the rider, puzzled.

"Did I say anything about Gunsight?"

"No."

"Or did I make any threats?"

"Threats? No, I don't recollect no threats."

Knight moved his eyes for a fraction of a second. They settled upon Arthur Hobart's hawk-like, dark, and bleak features.

"I don't like men putting words into my mouth, mister," he said, in a very quiet way. "You're Hobart, aren't you?"

"I'm Arthur Hobart. Who the hell are you and what are you talking about?"

"About a message you said I sent to the folks in this town, Hobart. My name is Ben Knight."

The room became tomb-like. No one moved anything but their eyes. Not a word was spoken for a long time.

Then Arthur Hobart twisted to face Knight, saying: "Mister, you got a lot of guts coming in here like this."

"Enough," Knight said, watching dark color stain Hobart's face. "If you want to call me out . . . go ahead."

Morgan Hyatt, watching Knight's unblinking gaze, read death there. He inched back as far as he could behind the bar, then he said: "Listen, Mister Knight, you're biting off a pretty big bite. These other fellows work for Mister Hobart."

"Thanks," said Ben Knight shortly. "I'd already figured that."

"Then," said Arthur Hobart, "maybe you'd better just turn around, tuck your tail, and get the hell out of here."

"You're kind of stupid," Knight said in reply. "I counted the horses hitched to the rack outside. Five of 'em. They all have your Diamond H mark on 'em. I knew how many men you had with you, Hobart, when I came in here."

This left the motionless men in the saloon to draw an obvious conclusion—knowing the odds he faced, Ben Knight had still come in. This meant he was either the biggest fool in the world—or confident he could down four men in a shoot-out. Either way, Morgan Hyatt and the few other disinterested spectators thought Knight was dangerous.

For a moment there was no sound in the Cross Timbers. Outside, in the southward distance, a dog barked and a horse whinnied. Reddening sunlight struck the saloon's front wall, puddling upon the scuffed floor where it passed across a window sill.

"You better leave," Hobart said, eyes drawn out

narrow, uncompromising mouth flattened. "You don't stand the chance of a snowball in hell."

Knight shifted his weight and he spread both legs slightly, standing clear of the bar. "I think I do," he answered. "It's you who's in my line of fire, Hobart. You'll be the first to go down. If your boys get me afterward"—Knight shrugged—"you won't know about it."

This was obvious to everyone. Arthur Hobart stood less than fifteen feet from Ben Knight. Behind him were his Diamond H riders.

Hobart also understood this, and he knew, as fast as he was with a handgun, this tall, self-assured man before him was faster. Hobart knew this instinctively, but he also knew it factually. He was balancing upon the brink of his grave.

"All right," he said. "What is it you want?"

"I want you to tell the men in this room that message you said I sent to Gunsight was a lie."

"What message?"

"Don't stall with me," said Knight. "I'll kill you, Hobart, as sure as you're standing there."

"I won't draw against you," the owner of the Diamond H Ranch said.

Knight's hard stare turned slightly ironic. To the men behind Hobart, he said: "How do you fellows like working for a coward? You saw it with your own eyes and you heard him, too. Let me tell you something . . . a man who won't defend himself, sure won't defend you, either, if you get into trouble. Remember that, boys."

Behind the bar Morgan Hyatt was staring incredulously at Arthur Hobart. So were other men in the saloon and Hobart also knew this. Humiliation made his face flame but otherwise he continued to stand motionless, staring.

Knight said again: "Tell the men in this room there was no message, Hobart. Tell them you made it up."

"I think," the cowman said, speaking very slowly now, as though he was thinking ahead to something else, "you'd better convince my riders of that, Knight. They believe you sent the message. So do the rest of the folks hereabouts."

Knight considered Hobart's face for a long time before he spoke again. Then, speaking to Hobart's Diamond H riders once more, he said: "You hear him? You can guess the truth now. He's got something else cooked up and you boys that he brought to town are to be part of it. Well, remember that this man will not help you if . . ."

"Knight!"

It was Morgan Hyatt who had yelled the warning.

Arthur Hobart's ruse had worked. He needed an edge, he felt, to draw against the taller man. He had diverted Knight long enough to get it. Hobart was going for his gun, his talon-like fingers a blur downward.

There came a deafening explosion.

Morgan Hyatt, unable to see over the bar, sighted only the sudden eruption of black-powder gun smoke. He shot a look at the adversaries. Both were still as they had been, standing about fifteen feet apart, glaring fully at one another.

Then Arthur Hobart's knees sprang outward. He crumpled. His body made a solid sound as it struck the floor.

Hobart's stunned riders were like stone. It had happened too fast, and now there was nothing between them and Ben Knight but his naked pistol barrel with its faintly curling wisps of dirty smoke.

No one at the bar or behind it had seen Knight draw. At a poker table near the door three card players, who had no dispute with either adversary at all, nor any interest in their disagreement, had seen Ben Knight's draw, and they sat there now staring at him, eyes popped wide open, mouths slackly hanging, their faces ashen.

"Knight . . . ?" Morgan Hyatt said tentatively.

"Yes."

"Someone better go for a doctor."

"No need," said the tall man, watching the Diamond H men. "He's dead."

Hyatt subsided. Very gradually some of the trauma passed. Somewhere out in the roadway and southward a man's high cry of alarm echoed.

That solitary gunshot had been loud enough; people had heard it. But except for that one cry, the roadway beyond Hyatt's saloon remained utterly deserted. None of the curious or the morbid rushed up as people customarily did after a shoot-out, to ogle victor and vanquished.

"Pick him up," Ben Knight said to the Diamond H men. "Take him outside, tie him across his saddle, and get out of town."

The cowboys moved at last, stiffly, awkwardly. They gathered up Arthur Hobart and lugged him across the saloon, shouldered past the spindle doors, and emerged into the empty roadway. There, while they worked at making their employer's body fast over the saddle, they spoke a little among themselves.

Finally, as they were mounting, one of them faced Ben Knight where he stood in the Cross Timbers' doorway, saying to him: "You didn't finish nothing, mister . . . you just started it."

Knight said nothing.

The horsemen turned away riding on out of Gunsight. They did not look back nor did anyone appear to stare at them. Where they wheeled easterly out upon the valley floor, they broke over into a wild race, Hobart's body jouncing soddenly along across its saddle, head hanging low upon one side, booted, spurred feet upon the other side.

Morgan Hyatt stood beside Ben Knight until

the last echo of hoofs faded out, then he leaned upon the log wall. "You better get astride," he told Knight. "And don't even look back."

Knight holstered his weapon and moved past as though he had not heard Hyatt speak at all. He had progressed perhaps twenty feet along the plank walk when he turned back to say: "Just whose side are you on, anyway?"

Hyatt shook his head. "Hobart had some cause to complain about the way folks here in Gunsight treated his riders. It wasn't all his making . . . this trouble."

"I see."

"No. Don't get me wrong, Mister Knight. The Diamond H is a tough outfit. They've ridden roughshod over folks here in town, too."

Hyatt drew off the wall, he squinted against the afternoon sun smash, looking down at Knight. He spoke again, and this time his words were quieter.

"But you didn't help anything, Mister Knight. Shooting Mister Hobart may satisfy you for something Hobart may have said about you that wasn't true . . . but Ace Dwinell is just as hard as Hobart was."

"Who is Ace Dwinell?" Knight asked.

"Hobart's foreman. He's got as little use for this town as Hobart had. Now, you fixed it so's Dwinell will sure as the devil want blood over Hobart getting killed here."

Ben Knight considered Morgan Hyatt a moment, then, in a tone that carried to Hyatt and no farther, he said: "You're overlooking something, Mister Hyatt. I have reason to hate this town!"

CHAPTER EIGHT

Ben Knight went to the livery barn. There, he ascertained from Cal Taylor who Colt Balfrey was. He then departed in search of Balfrey, who was an itinerant cowboy and saloon swamper. But he had been gone only a few minutes when Bob Hogan appeared at the barn. Ordinarily Hogan would not have come on duty as night man until somewhat later, but the news of Hobart's killing and the growing tension—plus his own secret anxieties—had drawn Hogan uptown like a magnet.

Now, Calvin Taylor told him of Knight's questions, and as soon as Colt Balfrey's name was mentioned, Hogan knew discovery was imminent, for Colt Balfrey was one of the weaker of Hogan's lynchers. He waited, affecting interest but a lack of concern personally, until Cal retreated to the harness room. Hogan then left the barn by the back entrance, fading out southward in the direction of Balfrey's shack, with lengthening shadows partially concealing him.

Knight, unaware he was being deliberately stalked, went directly to Balfrey's bachelor cabin at the southerly end of Gunsight. There, he found no trace of the man he sought. Behind Balfrey's shack stood a horse shed. It was empty as well, although there was ample evidence of recent occupancy. Studying the tracks of a recently ridden horse, Ben Knight could tell from the dug-in places where steel horseshoes had slammed down hard into the earth, and that whoever had ridden that animal—and he had no illusions here—had left in a hurry.

It was too late in the day to track this man. Dusk would shortly be settling. Knight went back to the horse shed and turned to examining it and its contents. He found a dusty pack outfit, complete with webbed britching. He also found a wooden grain barrel and a number of rusty old bits suspended from nails. All the impedimenta of a lifelong horseman were here, and there were also several boxes of household goods which evidently had been stored in the horse shed for lack of room in Balfrey's little bachelor shack.

To Ben Knight's lawman-trained eyes, there appeared instantly one outstanding discrepancy. Although the grain barrel had recently been opened and closed—as evidenced by the disturbed dust on its top—there was a long-time accumulation of dust in the feed box affixed to the west wall of the horse shed's simple tie stall. Balfrey had not, then, grained his horse in a long time, and yet he had obviously been at the grain barrel.

For a while Knight stood in shadow considering this. He did not immediately examine the barrel, but passed thoughtfully out of the shed, took a slow-pacing turn around Colt Balfrey's yard, found no other animals out there to whom the missing man might have fed grain, then he returned to the barrel, removed the lid, and thrust one arm deeply downward. Grain covered the lower half of the barrel. Knight pushed through this, rummaging. His fingers closed upon something which was not grain and he drew it forth.

A small flour sack hung in his fingers. In it had been cut two eyeholes. The lower part of this obvious mask showed by wrinkles where it had been pinched down to fit inside a man's shirt collar.

Knight moved deeper into the shed's gloom to sit loosely upon a manger. He continued to examine the mask. No one had told him the lynchers of his brother had worn masks. To the best of his acquired knowledge no one who had seen the lynchers was now alive. Yet he knew intuitively why Colt Balfrey, this missing man, had used this mask.

He arose from the manger, carefully folded the flour sack, and pocketed it. There was nothing more to be gained by remaining here. He moved forward. Beyond the horse shed where descending dusk was beginning to obscure those far-away mountains, there was utter silence. This, to a man of Ben Knight's training, was immediately noticeable.

Any frontiersman, reared in an atmosphere of naturalness, remained attuned to the world through which he passed. It became his second nature to consciously or unconsciously gauge the moods, the colors, and the silences around him. Now, Knight was aware of something beyond the horse shed which a differently matured man might never have noticed at all—there was not a solitary sound out there. This was the time of evening when birds went to roost. The time when they sought out trees, underbrush, buildings, to settle in for the night. There was no sound at all of birds settling or making their garrulous roosting sounds.

It was too quiet.

Knight paused within the horse shed's thickening gloom. He tested the shadow world beyond where early dusk was moving in over the land. Danger was out there.

He thought immediately that Colt Balfrey had returned, had seen him, perhaps with the flour sack mask, and was now lying out there somewhere with a gun trained upon the shed's only doorway.

Knight made a leisurely examination of the shed seeking another way out. He found none at all, for, although the shed was roughly put together, it had no cracks large enough for a man to squeeze through. He then passed across to the doorless opening again, went low upon one knee, and strained for the hidden assassin he was certain awaited him. There was no movement, no man-like silhouette—and no sound.

He went still lower, pressed his body flat upon the ground to inch forward, and, hatless, peer around the moldy mud sill, exposing only a small portion of his face. He was not now seeking his adversary so much as he was looking for a bulwark which might protect him when he made the charge out of the horse shed he was determined to make.

There was, some distance ahead, between shed and house, a pile of cedar posts, evidently collected against the day when Colt Balfrey got around to erecting a corral. There was also a stone cairn type of an outdoor fireplace where a bachelor might boil his soiled clothing in a cauldron, which was the customary way for single men on the frontier to do their laundry. In first approaching the shed, Knight had noticed both these obstacles to a direct passage to the shed but had attached no significance to either at the time. Now, he wondered behind which lay his enemy. Knight felt in his gut that Balfrey had to be hidden by one or the other because there was no other place for a man to hide within accurate shooting distance of the shed.

Knight, annoyed now by the gloom which made it impossible to determine upon the ground where fresh man tracks lay, considered the two places. The stone cairn was closest to the shed, but it lay in a direction in which a routed gunman would have no additional protection. He thought it unlikely that a gunman would choose this barrier, for if he were compelled to break and run for it, he could be shot down easily since there was no additional protection to retreat to.

The pile of posts, on the other hand, was between Balfrey's shed and house. In flight, an assassin could depend upon the house to protect him. This then, Knight told himself, was where he would have taken position.

He drew up his legs, arched his back, dug in his heels, and palmed his six-gun. He breathed deeply for the space of several breaths, then sprinted toward the cairn as swiftly as he could.

Immediately a gunshot blew the silence asunder. Then came a second lancing tongue of scarlet flame. Unhit, Knight threw himself bodily behind the rock cairn's solid substance, twisting as he did so to catch sight of that second shot. He had, fortunately, made a good deduction. There *was* an assassin in the yard, and he *was* behind the pile of posts.

Knight snapped off a shot, saw a dagger-like cedar splinter peel off and fly into the air, and swiftly drew in his exposed legs.

Silence came again, thicker, more ominous than ever, to mantle the Balfrey yard. There was no called forward threat from the assassin. No warning at all, and former lawman Ben Knight knew from experience that this meant his enemy in the predusk had no intention of scaring him off. He fully intended to kill him.

Seconds dragged past on leaden feet. Knight remained cramped and waiting. Nightfall, he felt, was on his side. If he waited long enough, with the aid of full darkness, he could possibly crawl out and around the post pile and flank his unknown enemy.

But Knight was not the only one thinking ahead to eventualities. The assassin, too, recognized the need for an early kill, only he attributed this necessity more to interruption from townsmen who heard the shooting than to the advent of darkness. He accordingly took careful aim with his handgun at the topmost rock on the stone cairn and fired.

The rock burst under impact sending razor-like splinters in every direction, shrapnel-like. One struck Knight on the upper arm. He winced instinctively and pressed lower to the ground. He also thrust his handgun around the cairn and fired once, blindly, and heard this slug strike the house beyond.

Another shot came to fracture a rock. This time, though, Knight was uninjured; he was moving clear in anticipation. Before still another shot came from the post pile, he raised swiftly up, aimed downward, and fired three times, patterning his shots so that they effectively bracketed the post pile. Then he dropped down to reload.

Time passed again, with silence returning to the yard. Knight waited for what seemed ages, then, feeling darkness was down sufficiently, began to edge cautiously clear of the stone cairn. He made an elaborate and time-consuming crawl far outward, then began coming down behind the post pile.

It took nearly an hour for him to accomplish this, then, when he was in position, he fired three times rapidly, first to the left of where he figured the assassin must be, then to the right of that spot, then directly in the center. Before the echoes of these muzzle blasts had died out, Knight was hurtling forward. He landed upon churned earth realizing as he groped for the hidden gunman, that the man was no longer there.

Sometime, probably when Knight had been making his painful crawl, the assassin had fled in the night.

Knight reloaded his six-gun first. Next, he very carefully exposed himself. When no shot came, he then put out a hand to lean upon the uppermost post to assist himself in arising. This hand, when he drew it suddenly back to peer at it, had blood upon the palm.

One of Knight's shots had struck home.

He made a closer inspection of the spot where the bushwhacker had been. He could barely make out the boot tracks or the imprints of a kneeling man's legs. Finally, he collected six spent handgun cartridge cases.

Before leaving Colt Balfrey's yard, he had also determined that the blood he had found had probably come from a hand or arm wound. Most likely, in arising from behind his barricade, the assassin had done exactly as Knight had also done—he had stretched forth a hand to steady himself in arising.

Knight passed back around Balfrey's shack to the terminating plank walk beyond, and there he struck out thoughtfully back northward, toward Gunsight's main commercial square.

The town, as before, was unnaturally subdued. A stranger arriving in Gunsight at this time might not have sensed anything amiss because it was now suppertime, but no stranger appeared in the wide and empty roadway, and behind the doors of homes and stores this illusion of quietude and peacefulness deluded no one.

Knight made his solitary way as far north as Jacob Howell's saddle shop. He might have passed by, but here lamplight glowed behind the window and he turned in.

Old Jacob and his granddaughter Kathy were there, neither speaking, neither concentrating upon what they were doing, which was, for Jacob, the concluding chore of skiving the saddle seating leather he had earlier been working upon, and which for Kathy Howell was the rendering of bills at a small, scarred desk. They both looked up solemnly as the tall, dust-encrusted man entered. Both saw the tear in his shirt and the dull sheen of blood there.

Still without speaking, Kathy got up, passed around Jacob's bench, and poured a basin of water. She took this back to the little desk, put it down, and crooked her finger at Knight, saying: "Sit down here."

The tall man crossed over and sat down gravely. Kathy tore Knight's shirt cloth further and began to efficiently wash the injury, which was not serious, although the slash was fairly deep and had bled copiously.

Knight, seeing old Jacob's gaze upon him, lifted the outer corners of his mouth in a sardonic small smile and very solemnly winked.

"I went to see Balfrey," he explained. "He wasn't home. When I was ready to leave, someone behind a pile of posts bushwhacked me. It was Balfrey, I expect."

Old Jacob began wagging his head negatively. "Not Balfrey," he said scratchily. "Someone else."

"How do you know?" challenged the tall man.

Kathy answered him, working swiftly and speaking almost disinterestedly, almost casually. "Because Colt Balfrey is over at Doctor Parmenter's with a bullet through his lungs."

CHAPTER NINE

Doc Parmenter opened the door to admit Ben Knight. He cast a professional glance at the visible bandage upon Knight's arm, showing through torn cloth.

"Kathy Howell," he said, indicating the bandage.

Knight nodded, then said: "Where is Balfrey?"

Parmenter turned, jerking his head for Knight to follow. They passed across Parmenter's parlor along a gloomy corridor and into a small room at the rear of the house.

"There," said the medical man, standing aside and gesturing toward a still form under a blanket in the room's solitary bed.

By subdued lamplight Colt Balfrey appeared to be dead. Knight went close to stare downward. Balfrey's chest was shallowly rising and falling.

"Through the lights," said Parmenter, coming to a halt beside Knight. He then added: "From the rear."

Knight bent to peer into Balfrey's face. The injured man returned Knight's look. He was deathly pale and blue-lipped, but his eyes had an otherwise look of warmth and resolve.

In a voice scarcely audible, he said: "I know . . . who you are."

Ben nodded, saying dryly: "I reckon most folks

95

hereabouts know me by now." He perched gently upon the side of the bed. "Who shot you?"

Balfrey rolled his head upon the pillow. "I don't know," he husked. "I was riding."

"Riding where?" Knight asked.

"Just . . . riding."

"And . . . ?"

Balfrey was struggling with something. For a time, he was silent, his gaze tortured and indecisive, then he evidently came to a conclusion, for he said: "I know who it was. I didn't see him . . . but I know."

"Who?"

Knight leaned forward to catch Balfrey's answer. It came only after a final inner struggle on the injured man's part.

"He was going to meet me beyond town. I saddled up and rode . . . out there. When I passed a boulder . . . he shot me."

"Who?" Ben Knight insisted, bending still closer because the wounded man's voice was fading. "Who did it, Balfrey?"

"Hogan . . ."

Doc Parmenter touched Knight's arm. "That's all," he said. "Come along now." He urged Knight to his feet, led him back along the corridor to the parlor, and when he faced around, Knight saw the bitterness in Parmenter's face.

"I should've guessed," said the medical man. "I guess in time I would have anyway. He meant

Bob Hogan. He's night hawk at the livery barn."

"Thanks," Knight said, starting past, toward the door.

"Wait a minute!" called Parmenter. "I got a little more to say."

Knight turned. "I'm listening," he said, watching the older man rummage pockets for his pipe.

"Hogan's been in Gunsight about a year. He's a troublemaker, but more than that, he's handy with a gun. There are some that say he's been a gunfighter. I don't know about that, but I *do* know he misses no opportunity to stir folks up. He's a natural-born hater . . . a genuine troublemaker."

"Thanks," Knight said, again turning doorward.

Dr. Parmenter followed him out onto the porch. "Balfrey's horse brought him in," he said. "I'll try and get the rest of the story out of him . . . if I can."

"You think he'll die?"

"I know he'll die," corrected the doctor. "Ordinarily, I'd say he had an excellent chance of living. It's not unusual for lung shots to heal properly, Mister Knight. But Colt Balfrey's lost more blood than any man can lose and still live."

"So," said Ben Knight, "that'll make this Hogan a murderer."

"For the second time," Parmenter said, gazing out into the forward night, his voice softening. "Knight, don't kill him."

"What?"

"Don't kill Bob Hogan. If you do, you may

never learn who the others were. Balfrey probably will not live through the night. He won't be able to tell us. Hogan knows who the others were, so don't kill him . . . or you will never know."

Doc Parmenter squinted up into the tall man's face. There were unuttered words upon his lips. He seemed unsure whether or not he should speak them. Then he shrugged and spoke anyway.

"You're a man who uses a gun like it's a cauterizing tool, Mister Knight. I can understand that, but I don't necessarily approve of it. Hobart . . ."

"Yes?" the big lawman prompted in a quiet voice when Parmenter paused. "What about Hobart?"

"You didn't have to kill him."

"Didn't I? Were you there, Doctor?"

"You know I wasn't," Parmenter answered gruffly. "In my lifetime I've patched up maybe a thousand gunshots. But I haven't actually seen more than a dozen actual shoot-outs." The older man squinted upward again. "And do you know something, Mister Knight . . . not a one of those fights had to take place. Not a single one of them."

Ben Knight considered Parmenter's dusk-shadowed face. He thought of several answers to what the doctor had just said, but he gave only a short and not altogether unsatisfactory reply when he finally spoke.

"In my lifetime I've participated in more shoot-outs than you've seen, Doctor. I know that once men are set on gunfighting, nothing short of death will deter them."

"But does that make it right?"

"No," conceded Knight, "it doesn't make it right. But it makes it necessary to defend yourself. That's the way it was with Hobart. He did his damnedest to get this town up in arms against me. Why he did that . . . I don't know yet. But he did it. I defended myself by asking him to tell the truth."

"Or draw his gun."

"Yes."

"And when he drew you killed him."

"That's right, Doctor."

"And now," said Parmenter, "you're going to hunt down other men and shoot them as well."

"Whether they get shot or not rests with them. You have no law in Gunsight now, so . . ."

"Good night, Mister Knight," the doctor said, turning shortly, passing back into his house, and closing the door behind himself with strong finality.

Knight crossed through Parmenter's rickety old fence, turned southward, and started along the plank walk. He stepped off into the roadway dust, ultimately angling toward Gus Cawley's livery barn.

Behind and southward, a light shone in Blakely's

Emporium. At the Drovers' and Cattlemen's Restaurant there were even brighter lights. Mostly, though, Gunsight was prematurely dark and silent. Those echoing gunshots from down by Colt Balfrey's shack had eloquently told the townspeople this strange and deadly duel was still in progress, and knowing, as they did, nothing about it or its participants, prudence dictated an attitude of watchful waiting—preferably from behind locked doors.

Knight paused in the formless evening outside Cawley's livery barn to take the measure and the pulse of Gunsight. He considered it likely the gunman who had attempted his assassination at the Balfrey place might still be stalking him. But he also thought it just as likely, since this man had been injured in their brief but heated exchange, he might be tending his injury.

Of two things he was reasonably certain. First, the assassin would not show up at Doc Parmenter's office, for obvious reasons. And secondly, he would not let their fight end on the indecisive note it had terminated with at the horse shed.

He then passed into the livery barn.

The wide alleyway was softly but adequately lighted by two carriage lamps, one on either side attached permanently to the walls. There was an even brighter light coming from the harness room.

Knight walked silently there. He stopped and peered into the room. A thickly made fat man sat at an old desk with his hat far back and a pencil in his mouth. He made sucking sounds while scowling fiercely upon some entries in a fly-specked ledger. Knight opened the door wide and passed into the room.

At first the fat man only growled without looking up. "Dammit, Bob . . . it's about time you . . ."

The fat man swiveled around, looked up, and let his voice trail off into heavy silence. He blinked, then arose to say: "Excuse me . . . I thought you was someone else."

"Where is he?" asked Knight. "That man you thought I was?"

"Hogan? Danged if I know, mister. He's supposed to show up around here by five o'clock."

"Was he here earlier?"

"Yes. In fact, he was here talkin' to my day man, Cal Taylor, a few minutes after someone was in here askin' about Colt Balfrey."

Knight digested this and came up with a conclusion. It had been Hogan behind that post pile. He had discovered, or guessed, both Knight's destination and purpose, and had trailed after Knight to protect himself.

"Where does he live?" Knight asked the man.

"At the boarding house behind the Cross Timbers Saloon."

"Thanks," Knight said, and turned away.

"Mister!" exclaimed the liveryman. "I guess it's no secret who you are, is it?"

"No."

"Then maybe I ought to warn you."

"I've already been warned, thanks," Knight said, resuming his way, passing completely beyond the office before the fat man spoke again.

"No, not about Bob Hogan," the liveryman continued. "About Diamond H. They're comin' to Gunsight . . . the whole crew of 'em."

"How do you know that?" Knight asked, having stopped to listen to what the man had to say.

"I rented a rig to a peddler. He was out to the ranch and seen Ace Dwinell organizin' Hobart's riders. He high-tailed it back to town, told me, got on his saddle horse, and lit out of here like a freshly cut calf."

Knight continued to stand gazing steadily at the liveryman for several minutes, then he said: "Are you a Gunsight councilman?"

"No. Dick Blakely is though. Him and old Jacob Howell and . . ."

"I don't care about who they are," Knight interrupted shortly. "Just get them rounded up here, and I'll be back in a little while."

"They may not want to come, you know."

"They'll come," Knight assured the man. "They'd better come, or they may not have any town by morning. I know what I'm talking about. I've seen this happen before . . . cattlemen turning on a town."

Knight left the liveryman standing in his harness room doorway, fat face creased with worry, thick mouth drooping at its outer corners. He re-crossed the roadway and started northward once more.

Night was closing over Gunsight now, its dripping obsidian-like substance touching everything. Knight felt less conspicuous in this protective darkness. He shot a glance skyward to estimate the time. From this knowledge he knew how long it would be before moonlight came. He had no wish to be walking these roadways after moonrise. After all, there was no safer way to murder a man from hiding than accomplishing this by night, and he knew that, now, Bob Hogan would not be the only one who would be plumbing the darkness for him.

He had no certain knowledge how swiftly Dwinell's crew would be organized, or how long it would be before they appeared in Gunsight. But he did know, having been to the Diamond H, that men of grim resolve could cover this distance in something under two hours, after they once started for town.

He assumed he had perhaps something over a half an hour to do what must be done before Hobart's cowboys struck town. He did not think he could do it in that short period, but he was determined to make the effort.

Some distance south of the Cross Timbers Saloon he passed the empty and unlighted office of Gunsight's former sheriff, and here a shadow came off the wall to accost him.

"Mister Knight . . . ?"

He had this man under a gun in less than a second. The shadow went utterly motionless. When next it spoke, its voice had climbed notches, so that it sounded almost shrill.

"No . . . I got no gun! Don't shoot!"

Knight did not lower his pistol. "Who are you," he demanded, "and what do you want?"

"My name ain't important," the shadow said swiftly, anxious now only to say what must be said then depart. "Someone down that there alleyway yonder wants to talk to you."

"Who?"

"Miss Kathy. She's the saddle maker's grand-daughter. She's waitin' down there for you, Mister Knight."

"Alone?"

"Yes, sir, plumb alone."

Knight holstered his weapon and said: "All right. Go on now."

He waited until the messenger had rapidly turned and struck out to the south, before heading for the little alleyway north and east of where he had been stopped.

CHAPTER TEN

He found her without effort, standing alone and patiently waiting. As he swung close, she said almost breathlessly: "Don't do it. Don't hunt the others down, Mister Knight."

"Why not?" he demanded of her.

"Because there will be too many for one man to fight. And there is another reason too. My grandfather sent a cowboy to Casper a little while ago to telegraph for a U.S. marshal to come here from Denver."

Ben Knight might under different circumstances have been diverted by this lovely girl's beauty. Now, though, while he certainly was not unconscious of it, he felt impelled by the necessity for swift action, to leave, to walk out of the alleyway's dark protection, and push his search for Bob Hogan.

"If the marshal comes," said Kathy Howell, thinking from his silence she was making her point, "he could be here in another two days."

Knight, who had recently made this trip himself, knew it took much longer than two days. It actually required nearly a week of steady riding to reach Gunsight from Denver. He shook his head at her.

"It takes a week of riding to reach Gunsight

from Denver, Miss Howell. I know because I just made that trip." He squinted down at her. "Tell me the real reason you don't want me to find those men?"

"I *do* want you to find them," the beautiful girl said insistently. "But not alone. Not like you're doing now. They'll kill you."

"And . . . ?" prompted Ben Knight.

Kathy Howell strained to see his face in the gloom. "And . . . ," she said, her voice turning solidly hard now and then stopping. "Because you will be as much a murderer as any of them, Mister Knight. Please, for that reason alone, don't go through with it. Please."

His gaze softened on her. "I'm not going to murder anyone," he told her. "If the men who lynched my brother fight . . . then I'll kill them. That is not murder, Miss Howell."

"It *is* murder," she insisted. "You'll force them to fight and you'll kill them. Morgan Hyatt and several others told us how easily you out-gunned Arthur Hobart. You comply with the laws of self-preservation, but actually you know when you challenge these men, that you can outgun them. That's murder, Mister Knight, pure and simple."

He shrugged. "Have it your way," he said, a little impatiently. "Maybe, if you had some kind of law here, I might not do it this way. Since you haven't . . . and since not a one of you has made any attempt to punish my brother's killers . . . I reckon I'll handle it my way."

"You're a lawman, Mister Knight. The town council would be very pleased if you would take over Mike Mulaney's badge and office."

"No thanks."

Kathy studied him briefly, and when next she spoke her voice was bitter toward him. "No, of course you wouldn't. You want to avenge a murder with more murders. You couldn't take Mike's badge because it would put restraints on you."

She turned abruptly away from him as though to go east down the alleyway. He caught her arm and faced her around. They were standing quite close.

"Listen to me," he said roughly. "When a town lets murderers go free, they kill again. I know. I've been a lawman for a long time. I've seen every kind of a killer there is. The worst kind are those who kill from hiding, from behind masks. They are cowards. When you encourage a coward with leniency, he thinks he is brave . . . but there is nothing on this earth more deadly than a deluded coward. You ought to thank me for what I'm doing."

He let go her arm, spun away, and passed swiftly up the alleyway toward the yonder plank walk.

Behind him, vaguely silhouetted in the gloom,

Kathy Howell did not move until, as Ben Knight thrust outward into Gunsight's broad roadway, a crashing gunshot blew the night apart with reverberations. She saw Knight stagger, lurch, and go down. She ran toward him. Before she was even close, Knight's handgun was up and firing, lancing the darkness with red flame. Then silence came, deeper than ever.

When Kathy got up to where Knight had fallen, he was not there. She burst clear of the alleyway and halted. Instantly a powerful arm had her, swept her off her feet, and slammed her roughly against a log wall.

"You idiot," Knight's harsh voice flung at her. "You want to get killed?"

Being knocked nearly breathless, she said nothing. Against Knight's rigid arm they could both feel the thunder of her beating heart. Then, very gradually, he took away the arm, drew up to his full height, and, still holding his cocked gun, peered narrowly the full length of the roadway. She heard a deep breath sweep into his lungs then out again. He holstered his pistol.

"Are you hurt?" she asked.

"I've felt better," he growled, without looking at her.

She watched him turn next to examining a glistening furrow along his ribs.

"You're shot!" she exclaimed, and would have moved forward, but his voice halted her.

"Never mind that," he said to her. "Come on. I think I might need you now."

She followed him dutifully back into the alleyway, saying nothing. She had almost to run to keep up with his thrusting long stride. He led her nearly to the southernmost extremity of Gunsight, then westward again up a dog-trot to the roadway plank walk. Here, far south of where he had been dry-gulched, he paused only long enough to make certain it was safe to do so, then, taking her hand firmly in his fingers, he sprinted across the empty roadway, across the yonder walkway, and down another dog-trot which left them in the far alleyway that traversed Gunsight's westerly stores and buildings. Here, he let go her hand and stopped. She was panting from the run.

He ignored her now as he carefully placed a handkerchief across the ragged flesh along his ribs where an assassin's bullet had nearly put a finale to the gunfighting career of Ben Knight. When the blood was at least temporarily staunched, he muttered: "Come on." Then he started her northward up the alleyway. Kathy dutifully followed.

They made steady progress with only the echoes of their own footfalls around them until, as near as they could determine, they were approximately parallel with the spot on the roadway's far side where Knight had been shot.

Here, he went slower, feeling his way. When

he came to a very narrow spacing between two buildings, beyond which he could see clearly in the star shine the entrance to the opposite alleyway where he had emerged, he entered, passed quickly almost to the debouchment onto the front plank walk, then he stopped. Behind him, Kathy could see nothing at all. Knight stooped, caught hold of something, and lugged it unceremoniously out onto the roadway and dropped it. Then he stepped aside so Kathy could peer past him, and said: "Do you recognize him?"

She caught her breath. "It's Will Holt," she murmured.

"That accounts for two of them, then," Knight said, gazing upon the dead man. Then he shook his head. "This one was even more stupid than Balfrey."

"Stupid?"

Knight gestured toward the narrow passageway behind them. "He was in there. There's not even room enough between those two buildings for a man to turn around. When he fired at me, I saw the flame, naturally, so I fired back. The error he made was that he could not shoot, then duck away. Those buildings kept him stationary." Knight shrugged. "Some bushwhackers live and learn," he said, "and some don't live long enough to learn."

Kathy frowned. "Is that all you have to say? You've just killed a man."

"Yeah," Knight acknowledged, beginning to feel pain along his side, his thoughts already turning away from the defunct assassin. "But I think he looks better lying dead over here than I'd look across the road . . . dead." He turned his smoky gaze fully upon her, saw the look of horror, and smiled at her, lips wide.

"Maybe I shouldn't have brought you along," he said.

"Why did you?" she asked haughtily.

"That's easy. I wanted you to identify this man. I wouldn't have known him."

He methodically unshipped his six-gun, chucked out two empty casings, and refilled the cylinder from his shell belt. As he did this, he said: "Miss Howell, who was Will Holt? Who were his friends?"

"He . . . Will Holt was a local rider. He worked for the big cow outfits from time to time. That's about all I know about him except . . ."

"Yes?" Knight pursued.

"Except that he drank a lot."

"What about his friends?"

"I didn't know him that well. I've seen him with Colt Balfrey though."

"Anyone else?"

Kathy moved back so that she would not see the body. "I can't remember exactly. . . . Oh, wait. There was Slim Evans. I've seen him with Slim."

"Who is Slim Evans?" Knight asked.

111

"He works as a handyman around Gunsight. People say he's simple-minded."

"Do you think he is, Kathy?" It was the first time he had called her by her Christian name. He turned to look down into her face.

The night light softened the hard look of resolve he had.

She nodded. "Yes, I think he is. I've known Slim since we were children. He didn't graduate from elementary school. He was still playing with hoops and wooden dolls when the other boys were playing baseball and going hunting. Slim has always been good-natured, as far back as I can remember."

"Yeah," Ben Knight said with irony. "Good-natured simpletons are easily influenced. Tell me . . . where does Evans live?"

"I won't tell you," Kathy said, with sudden spirit. She turned north and began to walk swiftly along.

For just a moment Knight was nonplussed. Then he rushed after her, brushed fingers over her arm halting her, and said: "I'm not going to kill Evans. I just want to ask him some questions."

"I don't believe you," she flared at him. "You just killed Will Holt. And I think possibly, because of you, somehow, Colt Balfrey is also dead."

"Kathy," Knight said in protest. "I didn't even know Colt Balfrey. As for Holt . . . you *saw* him try to assassinate me. What was I supposed to do . . . just stand there and be shot at? Listen, Kathy, I'll give you my word, I won't shoot Evans."

"No. If he drew a gun against you, you'd kill him."

Knight blinked. "Well, damn it all, a man's got a right to . . ."

"Not," interrupted Kathy angrily, "when he's forcing the issue."

Big Ben Knight's mouth hung ajar. He sucked back a mighty breath and expelled it with a head wag. "You tell me where he lives, and I promise you I won't lift a finger to hurt him. You got my word, Miss Howell."

She appeared to momentarily consider this, then she said: "I don't know how good your word is." He flushed and she saw this even in the silvery night and rushed on. "So I won't tell you where Slim lives . . . but I'll guide you there."

Giving him no chance to speak, she turned, beckoned, and started off along the walkway.

Knight's brows drew downward. He hesitated a moment before following her. It was in his mind to protest, to overpower her will with his own force and power. But, watching her ramrod straight posture as she moved along, he had an inkling that he might not succeed in this, so in the end he went trailing along behind her, a tall, large and very deadly shadow for so small and shapely and lovely a girl.

CHAPTER ELEVEN

Slim Evans had a small shack east of town. It sagged wearily and appeared to be quite old, like other shacks on Gunsight's outskirts. Some of these small buildings, having been abandoned, were taken over by men like Evans, who worked as handymen around the town, made habitable, and became residences by reason of occupancy. There was no vested title and a resident might move out as suddenly as he had moved in.

The Evans shack had a mound of carefully collected scrap iron out front. It was utterly worthless, but Evans, like others of his kind, had an overwhelming penchant for collecting things.

Kathy picked her way carefully around this heap of twisted metal, made her way to a door, beyond which showed lamplight, and raised her hand to knock.

From over her shoulder came the arm of Ben Knight to catch hold of her fingers. "Not just yet," he breathed into her ear.

He moved slightly away to peer into a grimy window. Within the shack, clearly visible, was a tall, gaunt man working at a cook stove. He wore no six-gun and his back was to the door. Knight returned to Kathy, saw her quizzically watching his expression, reached forward, and opened the door without knocking.

The man at the stove turned toward the door in a flash. He saw Kathy first and instantly smiled. Then he saw Ben Knight and his eyes darkened with apprehension.

"Easy," said Ben Knight. "Just stand easy."

Knight closed the door after himself, shot a look around for firearms, saw none visible, and went closer to the stove. Kathy, standing back, was watching him.

"My name is Knight," he said, "and you're Slim Evans."

"Yes," husked Evans, his voice scarcely audible, and fear like a banner in his gaze. "I'm Evans. I know who you are, too, mister."

"Fine, Slim. I want you to answer some questions for me."

"No," Evans said, shooting his gaze past Ben at Kathy. "I ain't goin' to. I know what you're after and I don't have to tell you nothin'."

"Colt Balfrey is dead," said Knight.

"Colt?"

"Yes. And Will Holt is dead, too, Slim."

Evans leaned upon the wall, his mouth hanging slack, and his fear-scored eyes nearly black as he stared at Ben Knight.

"Bob Hogan's in bad trouble, too." Knight nodded toward Evans. "Now it's your turn."

"You goin' to shoot me?" asked the quaking

man, saliva forming at the outer edges of his lips. "Don't do it, Mister Knight. I didn't want to go along with them. I didn't hardly know that fellow. Bob said we had to do it."

"Had to . . . why?"

"Well," mumbled Evans, "he said we had to teach old Hobart a lesson."

Ben looked around at Kathy where she still stood by the door. He said nothing at all, but he did not have to. The girl was watching Slim Evans.

Now she said: "Slim, please tell me what happened that night."

"I don't think I better, Miss Kathy," Evans said, and jerked his head sideways indicating Ben Knight. "He'll kill me if I do."

"No, he won't, Slim. He gave me his word he wouldn't."

"You plumb sure, Miss Kathy?"

"Plumb sure, Slim."

Evans gradually relaxed upon the wall. He eventually faced Ben Knight again. "You give your word now," he said in an admonishing way. "You got to honor your word, Mister Knight. You can't shoot me now."

Ben nodded.

Evans swallowed. He looked closely at them both again, then he began speaking. He told the story of the lynching as exactly, as precisely and vividly as it had happened. When he finished speaking, he ran nervous palms down his trouser legs, waiting.

Kathy spoke first. "Bob Hogan, Colt Balfrey, Will Holt, Frank Bell, and you. Are you sure there were no more, Slim?"

"Plumb sure, Miss Kathy. I was right there. I'd have seen 'em had there been others."

"And it was Hogan who shot the sheriff?"

"Yes ma'am, Miss Kathy. It scairt me pretty bad when he done that. It scairt the others, too. Hogan told us the town would thank us for hangin' that feller. We figured it would, too. But when Sheriff Mike got shot . . . well, that was different. Folks wouldn't like that at all. Sheriff Mike was . . ."

"Where's your mask, Slim?" Ben Knight cut in to ask.

"I burnt it," Evans replied instantly. "Hogan told us to burn 'em."

Ben removed the flour sack from his pocket and shook it out to hold it up. "Who wore this one?"

Evans and Kathy stared. Kathy in astonishment. Slim Evans in fascination.

"I don't rightly recollect, Mister Knight. All them masks looked alike. We made 'em out of . . ."

"I know," Knight said, putting the mask away again. "Slim, hang around town for a few days, will you?"

As Knight said this, he began to frown thoughtfully. Then, before Evans could reply, he

118

said: "On second thought . . . I have a better idea. I'll lock you up in Mulaney's office."

"Lock me up, Mister Knight?"

"If Hogan or the others learn you've named them, Slim, they'll hunt you down and kill you. You can see that, can't you?"

Whether Evans could understand this or not he did not say, for at that moment Kathy smiled at Evans.

"Please trust us," she said, and Slim reddened violently.

"I always did trust you, Miss Kathy," he mumbled. "I reckon you're right about the others, too. They'll try and shoot me for namin' 'em. Hogan told us never to ever talk about that there lynchin' with anyone as long as we lived." A random and irrelevant thought came to Evans. He gazed at the rusty stove. "Will I get fed in jail?"

"Yes," Ben Knight assured him, feeling pity for this gaunt man with the troubled face. "You'll be fed as often and as much as you like, Slim."

"That's good because that there stove don't work about half the time."

Knight looked across at Kathy. "Let's go," he said, and crossed to the door, opened it, and held it for them both to pass out.

On their way to the sheriff's office Ben and Kathy were particularly aware of the silence of this night. The only visible light was shining into the dark roadway from up near Gunsight's northernmost extremity. The light came from the Cross Timbers Saloon, in fact, where a few saddled horses stood drowsily at the hitch rail. But even there, where noise and music ordinarily echoed over the town, not a sound was audible.

Ben had to light the lamp on Mike Mulaney's desk to find keys to the strap-steel cells.

This light drew Richard Blakely and Jacob Howell. Old Jacob was carrying a short-barreled old .45-70 carbine in the crook of his arm and his seamed face was grimly set in an uncompromising manner.

When he caught sight of Kathy though, he went loose with relief.

"Thought you'd been carried off," he told the lovely girl. "You scairt me nigh to death, girl."

Kathy explained to her grandfather what had transpired. Jacob and Blakely listened to this recital with interest, then turned to watch Knight lock Slim Evans in a cell.

Speaking to Kathy in a tone too soft for Knight to hear, Blakely said uneasily: "I thought he wanted to kill the lynchers."

Kathy, also gazing at Ben Knight, said in a voice equally as quiet: "There is much more to this man than you think, Mister Blakely. Tell me . . . do you know what happened to Mike Mulaney's badge?"

"Why yes. I've got it right here. I've been carrying it around, hoping to find someone to . . ."

"Will you give it to me, please?"

The badge was passed from Blakely to Kathy Howell.

While her grandfather and Blakely watched, she crossed to Ben Knight, turned him toward her with both hands, then stood very close while she pinned the badge to Knight's shirt front. She did not raise her eyes or speak until she had finished, then she stepped back to shoot a look up into his face.

"I've helped you twice now," she told the frowning tall man. "You can do this much for me."

"Ma'am," Knight began, his voice flatly antagonistic, "I told you I wanted to do this . . ."

"Please, Ben. . . ."

Knight, caught and held by the violet eyes, hearing the plea in this beautiful girl's voice, and sensing behind her the impassively watchful and hopeful looks of the older men, hesitated, and in that moment, he was lost, for Kathy was again appealing to him.

"You aren't going to challenge them, Ben. You have Slim in jail. You know who the others are. And now you are the law in Gunsight. The entire town will support you. For your own sake . . . and for mine . . . please do it this way."

Ben Knight's features softened with a little wry

smile. He was on the verge of speaking when Jacob jumped in first.

"I know you got no call to love Gunsight, boy," he said, "and I don't rightly blame you for the way you feel, but you can save this town and no one else can."

Ben looked quizzically at old Jacob.

"Diamond H is coming to burn us out. Gus Cawley told me Dwinell was bringing the crew and didn't anyone have to tell me why. I was there the night Hobart said he'd burn Gunsight." Jacob paused to let this sink in, then he said: "And, boy, except for you it might not have happened. You shot Hobart, remember."

Knight made a broad gesture of resignation and dropped both arms to his sides. To Richard Blakely he said: "Do you swear me in?"

Blakely looked puzzled. "I don't know how," he said. "Mike always wrote the oath out and I just read it back to him."

Jacob grounded his buffalo gun and grunted. "Never mind that monkey business," he growled. "You're the law in Gunsight from here on . . . amen." He squinted at Blakely. "You second the motion?"

"I second it," gravely intoned the merchant.

"That's it, then," said old Jacob, then he fastened a stern look on his granddaughter. "Now you go home," he told her, and stay indoors. And just for once don't argue . . . do like I say, girl."

Kathy considered her grandfather over an interval of impassivity and silence, then she smiled at him. It was a smile that would have melted stone. She demurely murmured: "Yes, Grandfather."

Ben Knight's repressed smile showed less on his face than in his eyes; they twinkled down at the girl. "Do you always get what you want?" he asked her. "I didn't want to wear this badge."

For a long second Kathy looked gravely at Knight. Then, very slowly she flushed. "Not always," she said, turning away. "Grandfather, are you coming with me?"

Old Jacob snorted. "You need me to protect you about like a grizzly bear does, young lady. You just get on home, lock the doors, and keep away from the windows."

None of them spoke until Kathy crossed to the doorway, halted to gaze quickly back at Ben Knight, then passed from sight.

Richard Blakely cleared his throat. "What do you propose?" he asked Knight. "You're experienced at things like this, I take it."

"I've had a little experience," the lawman said dryly, turning a sardonic gaze on Blakely. "Go get Hyatt from the Cross Timbers Saloon."

Blakely looked blank. "You mean Morgan Hyatt?"

Knight nodded. "If that's his name, yes. He owns the Cross Timbers, doesn't he?"

"Yes," answered Blakely in a protesting way. "But Hyatt's a friend of the cowmen. He won't help us. . . ."

"Just go get him, will you?"

Jacob rumbled aside at Blakely: "Do like he says, Blakely."

Blakely departed, but his bearing loudly proclaimed that he thought what Ben Knight wanted was pointless and futile. After he was gone, old Jacob went to a chair and folded into it with the .45-70 balanced over his knees.

"Morgan's a good man. So are some others here in Gunsight," he informed Knight. "You aim to make up a posse and meet Diamond H with it?"

"Yes."

Jacob nodded over this and pushed tiredly up out of the chair. "All right. I know the fellows hereabouts who won't stampede when the shooting starts. I'll go round 'em up."

"I'd appreciate that," said Knight, watching the old man cross the sheriff's office.

"A question I'd like to ask you," said Jacob. "You still figuring on gunning those fellows who lynched your brother?"

Knight touched the badge he now wore, saying: "Not as long as I'm wearing this."

"Do you know who they are?"

"I know. At least I know them by name."

Jacob looked at the floor a moment, then said:

"Kathy helped you find out where they were, didn't she?"

"Yes."

Jacob nodded brusquely and passed out into the yonder darkness. Behind him, Ben Knight went to the chair of defunct sheriff Mike Mulaney and sat down. He wagged his head. Nothing in Gunsight had worked out as he had planned for it to.

CHAPTER TWELVE

Events had made clear to Ben Knight why Arthur Hobart tried to make Gunsight hate him. Hobart had meant to burn the town as he once had threatened, but he had craftily planned it to coincide with Knight's arrival. By spreading that false tale of vengeance—or else—Hobart had made the townsmen acutely aware that Knight meant them great harm. Thus, when Gunsight was put to the torch, people would immediately couple this fact to Knight's alleged threat and blame him for firing Gunsight.

Sitting now in Mike Mulaney's office wearing the murdered sheriff's badge, Knight knew without any supporting evidence that Hobart and his crew would have worked diligently at spreading the story of Knight's having torched the town. As things stood now, Hobart was dead, and his riders, under Ace Dwinell, who Ben did not know except by sight, were likely to attempt the carrying out of their dead employer's wishes.

They would still fire Gunsight.

It was the imminence of this graver trouble which made him push his own reason for being in Gunsight into the background. But he did not mean to abandon it, either, and when Morgan Hyatt returned to the sheriff's office in company with Richard Blakely, Ben had worked both dilemmas into a dove-tailed plan of his own.

"Sit down," he told Hyatt, and waited until the saloon proprietor had complied before speaking again.

"You've been a rider," he said to Hyatt. "I know how you feel. I'm the same breed of cat, Hyatt. I'm not a townsman and I've always resented the way townsfolk take advantage of range men."

Morgan Hyatt squirmed but said nothing.

Ben spoke on. "I've been told all the trouble didn't lie with Diamond H. That a good part of it was caused by folks here in Gunsight."

"That's true," Hyatt said, speaking for the first time since entering the office.

Ben touched the badge he wore. "It isn't true any longer. As long as I'm wearing this, riders will get a fair shake in Gunsight. Do you favor this, Hyatt?"

"I do."

"Good, then you can help me make it come about."

"How?"

"Do you know a man named Frank Bell?"

"Yes."

"And I reckon you know Bob Hogan?"

"I do."

"I'm going to deputize you, Hyatt, and you're going to arrest them both and fetch them here to be locked up."

Morgan Hyatt scowled. He began drumming with the fingers of one hand on the arm of his chair. Finally, he said: "Were they mixed up in the lynching?"

"Hogan was the leader. Bell was a participant."

Hyatt's scowl lessened but his drumming continued. "How about the others?" he asked.

"Slim Evans is already jailed here. Balfrey is dead by now. Someone shot him through the lungs . . . from the back. Will Holt . . ."

"Is also dead," Hyatt said, arising. "I know. I heard about it."

Ben watched the burly barman pace the room. He said nothing, nor did he take his eyes off Hyatt until the roadside door swung open and several men ambled in accompanied by old Jacob, who was still carrying his buffalo gun.

Hyatt, too, stopped to stare.

Jacob pushed through and halted beside Knight's desk. After shooting only a brief glance at Hyatt, he said: "Here are your posse men. All good men, boy. I'll vouch for every man jack of 'em."

Ben arose but before he could speak Morgan Hyatt crossed to the desk with his hand out, palm upward. "Give me a badge," he said. "I'll bring them in."

Ben rummaged Mulaney's desk, found some dented deputy's stars, and gave one to Hyatt. He grinned. "I don't recollect the oath," he told the barman, "but you know what we want to accomplish here."

Hyatt grinned as well. Between the tall lawman and the burly saloon proprietor something warmly mutual passed. Then Hyatt lowered his glance to pin on the badge.

At this moment Jacob broke in. "Who you sending him after?" he demanded of Ben.

"Frank Bell and Bob Hogan."

"Well now," exclaimed the old saddler gruffly, "Morg's a good man, Sheriff, but it's been a spell since he's gun-tangled with anyone. Let's just send some of my boys here along with him."

Ben brought forth more stars. He selected from among Jacob's recruits the hardest-looking men with guns and gave three of them badges. "You're deputy sheriffs under Morgan Hyatt," he told them. "Go along with him and do what he tells you to do." His gaze ranged among them. "Any questions?"

One of the tough-set faces relaxed long enough to dryly ask: "You reckon we could get a drink on the house at the Cross Timbers if we mind Morg real good, Sheriff?"

There was general laughter over this. Then the men with badges trooped out of the office into the yonder night.

Ben waited until their diminishing boot noises faded out before he turned a speculative gaze upon the remaining men. "We'll need a rider,"

130

he said. "Someone who can ride beyond town, locate the Diamond H crew, then come back and tell us which way they're coming to town and how they are."

A younger man stepped up. "I'll do it," he volunteered.

Ben looked at old Jacob. The saddler made an infinitesimal nod of approval.

"Here's your badge," Ben told the younger man. "Be careful."

Accepting the star, this man said: "I'll be back with the information as soon as I can."

He then also departed, leaving seven men still in the office, including old Jacob with his buffalo gun. Jacob obviously had something on his mind but since he made no attempt to speak out, Ben did not urge him. He detailed the balance of his posse men to patrol the town in pairs, and as he passed out their badges he admonished them not to use their guns unless necessity made it mandatory. Then, when the last of the deputies left the office, he turned on Jacob.

"Something bothering you?" he asked the old man.

Jacob cleared his throat. He colored. He frowned fiercely at the tip of his .45-70 barrel and cleared his throat a second time. "I got something to say, yes," he conceded, "but this ain't . . . isn't . . . exactly the time to say it." He shot a quick, darting upward look at Ben Knight. "Now don't blame me, boy. I had nothing to do with this."

"All right, I won't blame you. What is it? We don't have all night you know."

Jacob muttered a curse. "Kathy wants you to come by the house." Seeing the fixed look Knight put upon him, Jacob rushed on. "I told her you was too busy to pay social calls tonight. I said to her . . ."

"Which is your house, Jacob?"

The old man paused to consider Knight's face. "You know where Doc Parmenter lives?"

"Yes."

"Our place is two doors north of there."

Ben Knight ran a hand over his jaw and heard the scratch of beard stubble. "I'm not exactly presentable," he mused aloud.

Jacob stood up, saying with a head wag: "A heap of things get by in the dark, young fellow." Then, shocked at his own boldness, he added: " 'Course, a fellow's got his job to do, too." Then, red-faced, Jacob took up his big-bore carbine and stood uncomfortably waiting for Ben Knight to speak.

All Knight said was: "Yeah." He uttered this in a dry tone as he started across the office toward the door. From a position half in, half out of the sheriff's quarters, he faced old Jacob. "Stay here and watch things for me. I'll be back directly."

Jacob nodded without speaking. He waited until the door closed behind Ben Knight, then he turned back to his chair, sat down, and placed the .45-70 across his knees. In the midst of a man's troubles, he privately thought, there seemed always to be a little ray of hope to keep him going, to encourage him, something he could look forward to. Thus, it always was in life. Nothing was ever so bad that it obscured that which promised to be better in the future.

When Jacob's son and daughter-in-law had been killed in a flash flood nearly two decades earlier, they had left behind the little child which old Jacob's life had gradually fused around. Kathy had been his salvation. He had for all those intervening years lived only for her. But lately, he had been troubled. He was very old now and she had grown to be very lovely. Without admitting it, he knew the parting was close. He must soon go one way, she must go another way. And yet, among all the men who had come courting, he had found none he had thought worthy. Not that he was actually a difficult man in this respect, but he clung to the old virtues. He wanted her to have a man who was brave and resourceful and honest. This fitted some of her past suitors. But also, being an old-time frontiersman, he wanted for Kathy a man who was not as glib as he was sound in judgment, and this, in an age of dawning erudition, was less common.

Now, he told himself, the ray of hope was shining through again. In the midst of great peril,

Ben Knight had appeared. He was all an old frontiersman could ask in a man. Maybe, with God's good help, he would prove the answer to Jacob's secret hope.

If beauty and desirability were determining factors, then Knight would find Kathy as attractive as Jacob knew she had already found his rugged good looks and quiet good humor.

He sat there in the sheriff's office with orange lamp glow softening those lines and planes which a harsh existence had indelibly stamped upon him, hoping with his full heart that this might be so. He was certain, too, that Ben Knight's breed of individualists was constantly getting scarcer in this world of steadily increasing sameness and regimentation.

His thoughts were abruptly scattered by the bursting inward of the office door. Several thick shapes pushed inside from the roadway, herding ahead of them two disheveled, unkempt men whose faces were askew with fear.

Morgan Hyatt shouldered past to gaze upon old Jacob. "We got 'em both," he said. "Where's Knight?"

"He'll be back directly," Jacob declared evasively, and gazed upon the prisoners. "They give you any trouble?"

Hyatt went to the sheriff's desk, sought and found a ring of keys, and took them up in one hand. "Bell didn't. He was in bed when we busted in on him." Hyatt looked long at Bob Hogan. "Bob there . . . he was saddling up to leave town." Hyatt tossed the key ring to a posse man and pointed to an unoccupied cell. As the procession started forward across the room, he sighed and looked back at Jacob again.

"You know who shot Colt Balfrey?"

"I got no idea," replied Jacob.

"Hogan."

"Hogan? You sure?"

"He told us he did. I reckon he thought that was why we were after him. Anyway, when he put up a little scrap, his shirt got torn. He's got a bandage around his left upper arm. There's a bullet hole under that bandage. We roughed him up and he said Colt shot him when they met out of town."

"Whoa up!" exclaimed Jacob, frowning after the posse men who were locking Hogan into a cell. "Knight and Doc Parmenter said Balfrey was shot from *behind*."

"I know," Morgan said. "That's what stuck in my craw. Colt was hard hit. He couldn't have turned around and shot Hogan, so Hogan got that bullet wound somewhere else. But notwithstanding, he *did* shoot Colt Balfrey . . . and in my book that's murder."

"I reckon I'd best go tell the sheriff," said Jacob. "You wait here, Morg. I won't be long."

Hyatt went behind the only desk in the room

135

and sank down. "I'll wait," he agreed. "Anyone come in with word about Diamond H yet?"

"No." Jacob started forward. "If word arrives, keep the messenger here until I get back with Knight."

"Sure."

Jacob passed out into the star-washed night. Around him, Gunsight was breathlessly silent. Southerly and across the roadway two men were leisurely strolling side by side. Where the light of a belated moon struck downward, there shone reflected light off deputy's badges on dark shirt fronts.

Jacob hesitated for only a moment longer to breathe in the perfumed night air, then ambled northerly, trailing his buffalo gun after him.

CHAPTER THIRTEEN

Jacob was an old man and he walked slowly. This night, heading toward his home, he deliberately walked even slower than usual and it was well that he did so, for the fates in which old Jacob believed were on his side this time, but they needed a little more time.

Ben Knight had found Kathy sitting upon a porch swing made of creek willows when he had earlier approached Jacob's house. She had arisen to stand in soft night light as he had swung up onto the porch to stop toweringly before her. He could not see past the shadowed darkness of her eyes, but there was no mistaking the gravity of her expression.

"How is your wound?" she asked him.

He had forgotten the scratch acquired in Colt Balfrey's yard until that moment. "It's fine," he assured her.

She turned slightly from him. "I don't want to keep you long, but sit down for just a moment, won't you?"

Ben sat. The old porch swing creaked under his weight.

Kathy eased down at his side. He was not

making this easy for her with his silence and his steady gaze.

"You know that we gave your brother a Christian burial," she said.

"Yes. I visited his grave in the night. Before I came into Gunsight. I knew . . . from the flowers . . . you folks had feelings."

"I heard a rumor that you said you hated Gunsight." Before Knight could reply, Kathy continued: "As my grandfather said, a person couldn't really blame you." She turned now to look into his face. "I'm not going to apologize for the town. I don't think anyone could rightfully do that, Ben. What I wanted you to know is that, even with the bad feeling here between the people of the town and Arthur Hobart's Diamond H Ranch, none of us would have participated in that lynching, even if we'd believed your brother had been Hobart's hired gunfighter."

She paused before going on. "Ben, I've lived all my life in Gunsight. I know these people. They've had reasons for disliking cattlemen. But they aren't murderers."

"I think I understand that now," said Knight. "A man in my line of work gets so that he can pretty well gauge a town when he rides into it, Kathy. And I didn't actually say I hated Gunsight. I said I had *reason* to hate it. And I have."

"Yes," she murmured, lowering her eyes from his face.

"As for the cattlemen . . . I've been told there's been cause for dislike on both sides. That's the way it usually goes when there's bad trouble." He leaned forward slightly. "The thing is, Kathy, neither side can exist without the other. Cowmen need merchants, and you folks need the cow outfits to support your town."

"That," she told him now, her voice growing stronger, "is exactly why I asked grandfather to send you up here. I wanted to impress that upon you."

He smiled. "You didn't have to do that. I didn't come down in the last rain."

She flushed. "I'm sorry. I didn't mean it to sound that way, Ben. I'm not trying to do your thinking for you."

He hung fire over his next words for a pensive moment, then said: "In a way, I'd like for you to do that, Kathy. No man is sufficient unto himself." He put out a hand to touch her. She did not draw away. "If two heads are better than one head, then one beautiful head like yours must equal two ordinary heads." His hand closed down over her fingers. "I gave you my word about Slim Evans and you doubted me. I want you to . . ."

"No. No, Ben, it wasn't like that, really. I was afraid."

"Afraid?"

"Yes. I feared you might destroy something.

I wasn't thinking only of Slim. I was thinking of . . . you."

"Of *us?*"

"Yes," she conceded huskily. "Of us. I didn't want you to do something that would destroy the respect I had for you . . . the admiration." She looked swiftly up at him as her fingers came gradually to return the pressure of his holding hand, and her face flamed scarlet in the porch shadows. He could not see that, but he could easily discern the sturdy beating of her heart where a powerful pulse pounded in her throat.

"I wouldn't have destroyed it, Kathy. But I'll be honest with you. I meant to challenge Hogan. I wanted to kill him. The others . . . the law could have them. But Hogan . . . no."

"What have you done about him?"

"Sent some posse men after him. Unless he got out of town, I reckon they've got him by now."

She looked down at their clasped hands. In a quiet voice she asked: "Can I request a favor of you, Ben?"

"Yes. Anything within my power."

"Stay in Gunsight. Be our sheriff here."

His face smoothed out a little, became less mobile now. "I am a lawman. I have a job in Denver, Kathy."

"It's not the same, though. There are lots of U.S. deputy marshals. But Gunsight needs a lawman. It needs the kind of lawman who isn't favorable to either the town or the cattlemen. It needs you, Ben. I can't recall this town ever needing your kind of a man as desperately as it needs him now."

He shifted his gaze from her face to the night beyond. There was a brooding thoughtfulness in his stare. After a time, just before she drew his attention back to her with hand pressure, he swung his head slightly to peer ahead in the direction of Gunsight's cemetery.

"My brother was the only living kin I had," he told her. "He's buried here. I reckon you might say Gunsight does have a hold on me."

"In your heart, Ben," she murmured to him. "He will always be in your heart. But life is for the living, and Gunsight has another claim on you, too."

He turned toward her. In that moment she freed her hand, pushed both arms upward, and drew him to her. His lips felt the sweet pressure of her mouth, and in a transformed second the run of his temper responded. He caught her to him, returned her kiss with a fire that drowned her passion and left her weak when she drew back to lean against the porch swing's willow-slat backboard.

This, for both of them, was a confused and confusing moment. Neither said anything for a while, then Ben put up one arm to draw her down into the curve of his shoulder.

"For a person no older than you are," he said

softly to her, "you understand a lot about life." He paused, then repeated her earlier words. "Life is for the living."

The moments passed with neither of them moving. Kathy, with hot tears just short of brimming over, finally said: "A woman's love and her worry about equal each other out, Ben."

"Worry? What do you mean?" He raised up just enough to peer down into her shadowed face.

"I wanted so much for you to bring peace to this valley, Ben. Yet, I know that to do that you'll have to go up against men whose views are so different from yours and mine."

He eased back again. Beyond, far out in the night, came the faintly heard sound of a running horse. "You can't hope to overcome all differences overnight," he explained to her. "Sure, there'll be differences. But as long as most folks in the valley are agreed on what is right and what is wrong, there shouldn't be any more *real* trouble here."

She sighed. A moment later she pushed gently clear of his enfolding arm to turn and look into his face. "Ben . . . ?"

He watched the laterally shining moonlight touch her face and spin its magic in her golden hair and bring forth the visible evidences of her womanly worth. He told her then that he loved her.

She was rigid for a long time, just watching his

face. Then she leaned across him, and again his mouth felt the coolness, the wonderfully tender and soft sweetness of her mouth. She afterward whispered to him an echoing of his own words.

"I love you."

He was raising both arms to enfold her when again came that distantly heard clatter of a running horse. He froze, listening, then very gently he arose bringing her up with him. They stood together listening.

"It's the man I sent to find the Diamond H crew," he said, knowing this had to be so. "Kathy?"

"Yes, I know," she moved back slightly. "Please be careful, Ben. Please."

He tilted her chin and lightly brushed his lips over her mouth. "I'll be careful. You be waiting."

He left the porch, struck the plank walk, and turned southward to pace strongly forward with loud echoes of his own footfalls preceding him.

Elsewhere in Gunsight there were a few motionless silhouettes of men visible. Something that had not occurred in recent days until Ben Knight had agreed to accept Mike Mulaney's badge.

Swinging into town from the north came the horseman whose oncoming hoof beats had alerted every waiting posse man that the long-awaited showdown with Hobart's Diamond H was imminent. This man on his sweat-shiny mount swung past Ben and reined down in a dust-spewing halt before the sheriff's office. He hit the ground and started over the plank walk.

Nearing the sheriff's office, Ben called out, which halted the rider in mid-stride.

"Hold it! What did you find out?" Ben asked as he hurried onward.

The horseman waited until Ben was closer, then spoke only as recognition came. "They're less than a mile from town, Sheriff. It's the whole cussed crew of 'em and Ace Dwinell's leading the mob."

"Armed?"

"Loaded for bear, Sheriff."

"How many?"

"Twelve by my count."

Ben started past into the office. "That's not enough to get sweated up about," he told the obviously excited rider.

"Hell," that young man protested, following Ben inside. "These aren't farmers on horseback, Sheriff. This is the Diamond H."

Morgan Hyatt, seated at Ben's desk, sprang up when Knight and the rider appeared. He listened to the messenger's words, then frowned worriedly at Ben. "That's plumb right," he said to Ben in support of the younger man's words. "The Diamond H is something to step softly around."

Ben, conscious of the posse men lounging around the room, their eyes now fully and alertly upon him, fixed Hyatt with a wry look. "How many times have you been with crews that braced towns on the cattle trails?" he asked.

Hyatt started to say something, then abruptly closed his mouth.

Ben grinned at him. "That's all right," he told the saloon owner. "I've been there, too. The point I'm making, boys, is that if Diamond H had nothing but top gunfighters in its crew, it still wouldn't have enough men to brace this town. Not," he added, looking around at the crowd of men, "as long as you are armed, deputized, and willing to defend your homes."

"We are that," growled a bearded older man. "I'm against killin' I want you to know, Sheriff. But I ain't against doin' it to protect my family."

"This town can ask nothing better than that," Ben said in strong approval. He faced Morgan Hyatt again. "You in accord?" he asked.

Hyatt nodded.

Ben sought out and found the messenger who had brought them news of Diamond H's closeness.

"Which way will they hit town?" he asked this man.

"From northward, like they usually do. They'll come into the roadway about where Hyatt's saloon is."

Ben faced the saloon man again. "Take these men up to your saloon," he directed, "and place

145

them in two ranks on either side of the road up there. Then, when Diamond H rides in, you call to them to hold up. You understand?"

Hyatt nodded that he did, then he frowned at Ben. "Where you going to be?"

"First I'm going to get Jacob to round up the deputies we've got patrolling town. Then I'm going to . . ."

"Where is Jacob?" someone asked.

Hyatt had an answer to this. "He went out looking for you," he told Ben. "I reckon he'll be along directly."

Jacob would, as Morgan Hyatt had carelessly said, "be along directly," but at that precise moment he was upon his own porch.

Kathy, within the solid embrace of Jacob's sinewy old arms, was doing something she had not done in a long time. She was turning to her grandfather for solace in the face of events she could neither control nor influence. She was not weeping, but with a heart as full as was hers, she was only a breath away from it.

Jacob caressed her head saying: "Honey child, this is something everyone has to go through sometime or other in their lives. They have to face up to the fact that life is largely what folks make it. But in order to make it right and decent and good, folks got to sacrifice and they got to take risks. You understand that, Kathy?"

146

"Yes," she murmured with her face buried against his chest. "I understand it, Grandfather."

"Then," he said, releasing her almost roughly, "you're grown up . . . you're mature. So, you go on into the house and you pray for your young man while I go downtown and see if maybe this old carbine and me can't sort of help the Lord along a mite."

CHAPTER FOURTEEN

Ben Knight saw Morgan Hyatt and his posse men on their way north along the plank walk before he left the sheriff's office himself, and he had no sooner emerged into the darkness than he was accosted by old Jacob. The saddler, with his face's grimness reflecting only the immediate situation, did not mention that he had gone in search of Ben, nor, for that matter, where he had done his searching. All he now said was: "Did you see him?"

"Who?"

"Bob Hogan . . . who else?"

Ben blinked at Jacob. Without another word he re-entered the office, crossed to the desk, and turned up the lamp. Next, he went over to the strap steel cages and passed from one to the other until he found Hogan, who had prudently taken advantage of the recent excitement in which he had been overlooked to lie upon the cell's solitary floor pallet where he was only barely visible.

At Ben's side, Jacob said: "You want the keys? I'll fetch them." Then Jacob pursed his lips, studied the sheriff's face briefly, and contradicted himself. "On second thought, I don't think I will." He plucked at Knight's arm. "Come on,

149

we've got work to do. This fellow will keep until later."

Ignoring old Jacob, Ben ordered Hogan to get up onto his feet.

This the prisoner did in a silence full of obvious apprehension. He did not cross the cell but stood back looking owlishly into Ben Knight's face.

For a time, the sheriff's unwavering and deadly glare was riveted to his brother's murderer. Then he abruptly turned away without a word.

Jacob followed him back out into the night and paused beside him upon the plank walk.

Without looking down, or apparently even thinking of Jacob at all, Knight said: "Round up the deputies who're patrolling town and meet me at the livery barn with them."

He then left Jacob to cross through the roadway dust and fade out in the general direction of the barn.

Jacob watched Knight disappear. He screwed up his face, scratched his head in puzzlement, then, with a shrug, started out to comply with the orders he had received. As he walked along he rationalized Knight's peculiar behavior by telling himself that, since he was not now and never had been a lawman, he had no accurate knowledge of how they worked under circumstances like these, and since there were times when you had to accept a man on faith, he must do this now. He must have faith in Ben Knight.

Morgan Hyatt, neither as old nor as philosophical as Jacob Howell, felt differently as he listened to the oncoming sweep of many galloping horses out in the night beyond Gunsight.

He said to the little cluster of men around him: "No shooting. No matter what happens here . . . no shooting."

The same older, bearded man who had spoken out in the sheriff's office gazed upon Hyatt now with a puzzled look. "They won't spend much time talking," he said. "Not Hobart's crew. There are gunfighters in it."

Hyatt mopped at his face. It was not a hot night, but he was perspiring profusely. He turned irritably upon the bearded man. "Listen," he rumbled loudly enough for all to hear him. "It's not going to be said we started a war here tonight, and you fellows remember that."

He craned his neck peering beyond, southerly down the dark and empty roadway. "Where is that damned sheriff?" he queried agitatedly. "Damn it all. I don't like this."

"I can see 'em," a man called from across the roadway. "Didn't that fellow who rode out say there was twelve of 'em?"

Someone affirmed this.

"I don't see but ten," said the informer. Look yonder."

They did not have to strain very hard, for the Diamond H riders were sweeping directly forward now, backgrounded by the far-away hills, becoming increasingly visible as they approached.

"Ten is right," said the bearded man, lifting his carbine off the ground and holding it across his body with both hands. "Go out into the roadway," he called quietly to Morgan Hyatt. "Sheriff Knight said to halt 'em."

Hyatt shot this man a hard look, then began moving out farther into the dust. His shirt was clinging to him. It was not that Morgan was afraid. He was no physical coward. It was simply that he had been maneuvered into a position which left him feeling as though he were betraying a trust, and he had done the job himself.

The dark body of clustered horsemen slowed to a walk as they entered Gunsight. Except for the gravelly sound of their horses' shod hoofs passing along, there was not a sound anywhere in the night.

Morgan counted them as they came close enough for him to see them clearly. There were, as the unidentified observer had noted, only ten riders. Hyatt had a moment to wonder where the other two might be, or whether the rider who had gone out to count them had not arrived at the wrong figure. Then he had no further time for private speculation.

A large-boned, rough-appearing man riding an equally tough-looking big bay horse whose high-crested neck and hammer head indicated that this animal was a ridgling, reined down to a halt some seventy-five feet away. He then sat there gazing from Morgan in the roadway to the dark and numerous shapes of other armed men on either side of the roadway.

This was Ace Dwinell, a man whose gun-fighting prowess had preceded him to Gunsight country, and in fact had been one of the reasons why Arthur Hobart had hired Dwinell as the Diamond H foreman several years before. He now brought his gaze back to Hyatt and spoke in an inflectionless tone.

"Hello, Morg. I see you got some townsmen here." The deep-set baleful eyes of Dwinell burned coldly against Hyatt. "Reckon Mister Hobart and some of the rest of us had you figured wrong. We always sort of figured you to be a range man."

"Listen, Ace," Hyatt said in a voice that gradually firmed up as its speaker resolutely faced the mounted men. "We don't want any trouble here. There's been enough bad blood on both sides. Unless this thing is stopped now, there's going to be more . . . and we don't want that."

"No," said Dwinell, crossing both hands upon his saddle horn. "I reckon you don't, Morg." Dwinell's sunk-set eyes glowed. "You spokesman for the town, Morg?"

"Well," stammered Hyatt. "Not exactly, Ace. I just happen to be here is all. Now listen, Ace . . ."

"Morg, you listen. That there Knight fellow killed Mister Hobart. Gunsight don't get away with that. Not by a damned sight."

"But that was a private fight, Ace. Gunsight had nothing to do with it. You got to look at this . . ."

"He's dead, Morg. He was shot to death in your town. Now you've went and made this Knight your sheriff. That's like pinning a medal on him for downing Hobart." Dwinell gestured to the bitter-faced horsemen sitting silently behind him. "That's the way us fellows look at it. Right, boys?" Dwinell's arm returned to his side. He rested his hand upon his holstered six-gun. "You take this fellow's side, Morg, you got to expect the consequences." Dwinell paused to let his words sink into the deathly stillness. He swung his head slowly from side to side, staring into the faces on both sides of the road.

After several minutes of silence, Dwinell added: "Mister Hobart told you townsmen what he was going to do if you didn't quit making things hard for the cowmen. Well, we're here to do it. Shooting him don't change that."

"Ace, you won't get it done," said Hyatt. "There aren't enough of you."

Dwinell studied Hyatt briefly, then shrugged.

"Maybe we won't have to do it," he said. "You

154

fellows just hand over this Ben Knight and we'll turn around and ride out. No one'll fire your damned town then." He sat there, waiting.

Morgan Hyatt turned to cast a desperate look around him for Knight. He did not see him. For that matter, he found that the other deputies who had been patrolling the town had not come up to support his little crew of townsmen who were facing Diamond H, and this as much as Sheriff Knight's absence sent Hyatt's morale plummeting.

He faced Dwinell to say: "Give us some time to talk this over, Ace."

Dwinell shook his head. "No dice," he stated flatly. "Whatever's done has got to be decided right now. Right here and now, Morg."

Hyatt looked over at the men on the east side of the road. His gaze fell unexpectedly upon Jacob Howell. The old saddle maker was leaning upon his buffalo gun with a serene and almost cheerful expression upon his face. This irritated Hyatt.

In an accusing tone, he said to Jacob: "Where in hell is Knight?"

Jacob deliberately drew back, took up his gun, and cradled it across his arm, then, with his free hand, he pointed. "Right over there, Morgan. Right over there with eighteen men, and every man jack of 'em has got a carbine sighted on these here hard cases."

For a moment, the men, both mounted and dismounted, gazed fully upon old Jacob. Then, a few at a time, they began to turn, following out the line in which Jacob was pointing. It was then that everyone could hear a hiss of gently expelled breath, almost like a sigh, pass outward from the Diamond H's mounted riders.

Barring Diamond H's withdrawal from Gunsight with their guns, fully athwart the roadway behind the mounted men, stood Ben Knight and his additional deputies. Diamond H had buildings to the east and west of them. They also had an overpoweringly strong body of armed men in front and behind them.

Into the ensuing fateful silence, Knight called up to Ace Dwinell: "You're asking me to go out of town with you. Well, I'll be happy to oblige. But it'll be just you and me alone, Dwinell, and only one of us will come back. Now, get down off that horse!"

Diamond H's foreman sat like stone, half twisting backward in the saddle to see Knight. He did not make a sound.

"I said get down off that horse, Dwinell!" Ben ordered.

Very gradually Dwinell moved. He swung one leg over the cantle and struck down into the roadway, facing away from Morgan Hyatt and his posse men. To Ben he said quietly, careful to keep his right hand well clear of his holstered, lashed-down pistol: "You won't settle anything this way, Knight. Mister Hobart said the town was to be burned . . . and burned it's going to be. With me or without me."

Ben, far enough back so that Dwinell's mounted companions could not flank him, stood wide-legged in obvious preparation for what lay ahead.

"I don't think so," he replied, in a tone as quietly resolute as Dwinell's voice had been. "Those two men you sent around to the west to start torching, are both in jail."

Diamond H's men looked gradually away from Knight to their foreman. Dwinell himself considered Knight over a long interval of silence. After several drawn out bad moments of this had passed, it was Jacob who spoke.

His words were addressed to the posse men around him on the plank walk, and they were easily audible to the mounted men. "That's the truth. Ben figured Diamond H would try it like that. He figured the big bunch of 'em would ride into town to hold our attention, while those other two fellows with the coal-oil cans would go out around town and commence setting fires. He had men watching and ready. That's what kept us from coming up here right away. Some of the local boys found both them fire bugs and packed 'em off to the jailhouse."

Pausing to let the words sink in, old Jacob

narrowed his eyes in a long, hard look upward at the listening cowboys. " 'Course, any you other fellows care to have a try at firing things up . . . why just ride on down the roadway and have a go at it."

As he said this, Jacob cocked his old .45-70. It made a sound so loud and convincing in all that otherwise stillness that not a doubt existed anywhere as to Jacob's meaning.

Morgan Hyatt turned a scowling countenance upon Dwinell. "That was a pretty underhanded thing to do," he said.

Dwinell did not reply. He was still watching Ben Knight with his undivided attention. Hyatt's last words echoed briefly, then the deadly silence pulsed on.

Finally, Dwinell spoke, and although none of the onlookers could see it in his eyes, there was in his stance the solid resolution of a man willing and ready to fight.

"All right, Knight," he said. "You called it. You and me will just walk out a ways and have this out." Dwinell still carefully kept his arm hanging wide of his holstered gun. "Unless your guts have run out through your boot soles while we been standing here talking."

Knight stepped back a short distance and jerked his head sideways. "Walk," he ordered. "I'll follow you."

Ace Dwinell began moving. As he passed his

cowboys, one of them called out to him. "What about us, Ace?"

"Just relax," replied the Diamond H foreman stonily. " I'll be right back. This won't take long."

CHAPTER FIFTEEN

To the men filling the roadway in front of Morgan Hyatt's Cross Timbers Saloon there was a bizarre awkwardness in the air. Dwinell's Diamond H horsemen sat self-consciously gazing about them. Ben Knight's organized townsmen, mostly bearing carbines and rifles, held their weapons loosely, an indication of disapproval with themselves.

Jacob Howell and one or two others, still resolutely grim and determined, kept hawk-eyed watch on the riders. Old Jacob reflected privately that trouble usually affected people in this fashion—as long as the tension lasted there were some who would persevere. But let reaction set in and most people were bothered by self-doubt, by procrastination and its accompanying demoralization. He saw this happen now as men muttered to those nearest them, looked uncomfortably at their adversaries, and made long and critical studies of the ground underfoot.

Beyond Gunsight in the depth of night, Ace Dwinell strode purposefully forward with Knight pacing behind him. When he thought they were far enough out, Dwinell slowed. Immediately Knight's voice hit him in the back.

"Keep walking. I'll tell you when to stop."

Dwinell went on.

They were a long two hundred yards out when Ben said: "Turn around."

Dwinell wheeled. He seemed, somewhere since leaving Gunsight, to have lost something. There was yet no fear or cowardice in his steady gaze, but his lips had softened away from their former harshness.

"You're making a mistake," he told Knight. "You're not bucking Arthur Hobart now, lawman."

They stood about sixty feet apart with dripping night between them. Each man stood gently sprung forward at the knees. Each man had his gun arm cocked for the blurring downward sweep. In the watery light they even looked alike. Both were above average in height. Both were strong-willed men without an iota of fear to them.

"Hobart," said Knight, "had some help along. You haven't."

"That kind of help," snorted Diamond H's foreman, "ain't no good anyhow."

For a lingering moment they regarded one another without speaking, then Knight said: "Back off, Dwinell. It's not too late."

Dwinell made the smallest of wags with his head. "I never backed off in my life, fellow. I'm too old to commence now."

"What's the point in getting killed?" asked Knight. "You can't stay in Gunsight country anyway . . . win or lose. So go back, get on your horse, and ride on. There'll be talk, sure, but it can't bother a man who is hundreds of miles away."

Dwinell's lips drew apart in a wolfish grin. "That's pretty good advice," he said in a drawling way. "Why don't you take it yourself?"

"I'm going to stay here, that's why."

"I heard you was a U.S. deputy marshal. That right?"

"That's right."

"What the hell can a hick town like Gunsight offer to a man like you, Knight? You just want a place to sit down and grow old in?"

Knight drew in a careful breath and expelled it. "That's about it," he replied. "You might give that some thought, too, Dwinell. We're about the same age. A man doesn't get any younger." Knight paused for emphasis, then added: "But he gets a little slower on the draw as time passes."

Dwinell's humorless grin lingered. He considered Knight thoughtfully, then said: "You going to talk me to death, fellow?"

"No. You can make your play whenever you're ready."

They had both said all they had to say. Actually more than either of them had meant to say. Among professional fighting men there was an imbedded, age-old conviction: the longer a man talked, the less likely it was that he would fight.

It was not possible for Ben to see Ace Dwinell's mouth because too much night gloom lay between them. Had this not been so, he would have strained to catch that slightest tightening of Dwinell's lower face which would have given him a fraction of a second's warning. Gunfighters did not watch an opponent's eyes—they watched his mouth.

Another second went by. It seemed as though all eternity was packed into it for one of them. Then Ace Dwinell went for his gun. There was nothing actually to see. His right shoulder scarcely dipped downward at all. His taloned fingers were a blur of speed.

Ben, as experienced as Dwinell—but more intelligent, and this made the difference—did not lower his shoulder at all. He was already standing hip shot so that his right side was lower than his left side. This was a slight consideration, true, but in a race against time for survival the most infinitesimal advantage was often the difference between life and death.

Ben had another advantage, too, but Dwinell could not have known of it. In fact, he did not even suspect it until, dead ahead and out of the darkness, came that rocketing muzzle blast with its accompanying red lash of flame. Then it was too late.

Dwinell's pistol exploded as Knight's slug struck him, half turning his body with impact. Dwinell's bullet tore up a gout of earth twenty feet short of where Ben Knight stood.

The wounded man forced himself back around. He stood weaving unsteadily like a tall tree in a storm, and he would have brought up his gun for a second shot except that his strength was too swiftly ebbing. He dropped the gun. His knees bent, and he slid heavily down to stretch his full length upon the ground.

Ben crossed to him and knelt. With dimming eyes, Dwinell said: "Hold up that . . . gun."

Ben complied, cradling the dying man's head with his free arm.

"Be damned," said Dwinell. Those were his final words.

Ben put his head gently back upon the ground and picked up the fallen man's six-gun. The pistol of Ace Dwinell had a regulation eight-inch barrel. Ben Knight's six-gun had had the barrel sawed off at four inches. Knight's advantage had been the difference between life and death. He had his weapon clear of its holster a fraction of a second before Dwinell's longer barrel cleared leather. On so seemingly insignificant a thing as that had a man's life depended.

Ben walked back to the straining, still, and stone-like townsmen and range men. Until he appeared, fully recognizable through the darkness, there was not a sound. After he appeared a sigh passed over the crowd. The sheriff of Gunsight had triumphed. That was what those waiting men wanted to know: who had been victorious.

Ben stood a moment gazing at the cowboys. They returned his regard owlishly. He then spoke to them quietly, and in a twinkling the tension dissolved.

"A man does what he has to do," he told them, now. "I have no regrets . . . but I think we owe a toast to the one of us who didn't come back. Dwinell was a brave man." He let that sink in, then added to it: "Mister Hyatt, I'll take it kindly if you'll pour the drinks for all of us . . . Diamond H and townsmen alike. I'll stand the bill."

Morgan Hyatt shifted position, shuffled his feet in the dust, looking up expectantly at the Diamond H riders. One of the mounted men put both hands upon his saddle horn, kicked his right leg up and over the cantle, and swung down. He was an older rider—a grizzled man with perpetually squinted eyes.

"I'll drink to that," he said, and at once the other Diamond H men dismounted to troop forward and hitch their animals at the Cross Timbers' hitch rack.

Around them the townsmen, more than ever self-conscious about the guns they carried, pushed those weapons out of sight against

Morgan Hyatt's front log wall and pushed into the saloon with the cowboys.

Ben, standing back until the others had entered, turned to face the man who came forward now to pluck gently at his sleeve.

"Well spoken, son," old Jacob murmured, his ancient eyes fully on Knight with strong approval. "It's never easy to kill a man, and usually, afterward, a fellow's got to live in his own private hell for a while." Jacob took up his buffalo gun, laid it across one arm, and nodded. "You go have that drink. I'll get a wagon and fetch Dwinell down to Doc's shed for cleaning up and laying out."

Ben had not one drink, but two. He offered no additional salute to the courage of the man he had killed, but those who, like himself, solemnly downed their liquor understood, for they, too, felt as Ben did. A man did what he had to do.

But he did say one thing before leaving the saloon. With his back to the yonder night and his shoulders filling the doorway of Morgan Hyatt's saloon, he called for silence. Then he said: "I'm not going to say Ace Dwinell died uselessly. But I am going to say if each one of you will turn around and offer your hand to the man beside you . . . and if you'll put meaning into that handshake . . . Gunsight and the cattle outfits won't ever have to go through a thing like this again."

He paused, watching the townsmen and cowboys look at one another, then he said: "Good night, boys." And he passed out into the roadway's stillness.

He had walked perhaps fifty yards south of the Cross Timbers when a creaking dray wagon went slowly past with old Jacob upon the seat. They exchanged a long glance, but neither of them nodded. Then Jacob was gone northward and Ben continued southward until he could distantly make out the bleached-bone white fence around Doc Parmenter's front yard.

He turned in two doors north of the Parmenter place and went up to the porch steps. She was there, waiting. At sight of his familiar silhouette she had arisen from the swing and swept to the porch's very edge to stop, looking down to him.

"Are you all right?"

He went to her, led her back to the swing, and sat down.

"I'm all right," he then said.

"I saw grandfather go by with the wagon."

"Yes."

She sat close, aware of their touching hips and shoulders. "I'll make us some coffee if you'd like, Ben."

"I'd like that, Kathy."

She made no immediate move to arise, and after a time she murmured to him: "Is it all over now?"

"I think it is, yes."

"And you will stay?"

He put forth a hand to touch her. "I will stay," he said, "if you will marry me."

She twisted fully toward him, saw the looming dark sweep of his shoulders blotting out the farthest stars, and met his lips with her own in a quiet kiss.

"I will marry you."

He drew back. There was a faint twinkle in his eye. "And now the coffee," he said.

She smiled mistily, arose, and passed around him bound for the house.

He caught her hand to draw her temporarily to a halt.

"Do you know that it will always be like this?"

"How do you mean?"

He let go the hand and looked gravely out into the dark roadway and beyond, as far out as the faintly discernible mountains rimming Gunsight Valley.

"Every time there's trouble here, you'll have to sit and wait . . . and wonder."

"Yes," she told him unsmilingly, "I thought of that tonight. But not always, Ben. There will come a time when conditions on the frontier won't be like they now are."

"I wonder," he mused, then roused himself. "Can I help you inside?"

She shook her head at him and moved on to disappear within the house.

He sighed. He ran his legs out their full length upon the porch flooring and allowed his body to turn completely loose where he sat.

From the north came a familiar sound of grinding wagon tires. Jacob was passing along slowly with his burden.

Someone struck a loud note on Morgan Hyatt's old piano up at the Cross Timbers Saloon. This note, discordant though it was, seemed to Ben Knight a kind of paean.

A few men appeared upon the plank walks heading northward. It did not take long for the word to pass, Knight thought. By this time tomorrow Gunsight would be well along on its road of recovery. Cowmen and townsmen would work at healing old wounds. A little effort was all that was required. But he knew it would take time.

Kathy returned with the coffee on a tray. She helped him with his and took the second cup to her seat at his side. She obviously had been thinking of things he had temporarily forgotten, for she now said: "What will happen to Bob Hogan?"

He sipped thoughtfully before replying. "Prison for life if he's lucky. Death by hang rope if he isn't."

She looked over at him. "You are not sorry for him, Ben?"

He answered truthfully. "I've never met a man

I felt less sorry for, Kathy." He caught her gaze and held it. "Does that shock you?"

"No, I don't think I expected any different answer."

"But you wish I was more sympathetic?"

She looked into her cup as she answered with a slow head shake. "No, Ben, I only want you always to be honest with me." She swept her glance suddenly upward to him.

He drained off the last of his coffee, set the cup aside, and regarded her with slowly widening and tender eyes. "I will be, Kathy. I promise you that."

He bent to kiss her. She turned fully to meet his mouth. The thin overhead moon sank behind a silvery cloud and for that moment darkness lingered.

ABOUT THE AUTHOR

Lauran Paine who, under his own name and various pseudonyms has written over a thousand books, was born in Duluth, Minnesota. His family moved to California when he was at a young age and his apprenticeship as a Western writer came about through the years he spent in the livestock trade, rodeos, and even motion pictures where he served as an extra because of his expert horsemanship in several films starring movie cowboy Johnny Mack Brown. In the late 1930s, Paine trapped wild horses in northern Arizona and even, for a time, worked as a professional farrier. Paine came to know the Old West through the eyes of many who had been born in the 19th Century, and he learned that Western life had been very different from the way it was portrayed on the screen. "I knew men who had killed other men," he later recalled. "But they were the exceptions. Prior to and during the Depression, people were just too busy eking out an existence to indulge in Saturday-night brawls." He served in the U.S. Navy in the Second World War and began writing for Western pulp magazines following his discharge. It is interesting to note that his earliest novels (written under his own name and the pseudonym Mark

Carrel) were published in the British market and he soon had as strong a following in that country as in the United States. Paine's Western fiction is characterized by strong plots, authenticity, an apparently effortless ability to construct situation and character, and a preference for building his stories upon a solid foundation of historical fact. *Adobe Empire* (1956), one of his best novels, is a fictionalized account of the last twenty years in the life of trader William Bent and, in an off-trail way, has a melancholy, bittersweet texture that is not easily forgotten. In later novels like *The White Bird* (1997) and *Cache Cañon* (1998), he showed that the special magic and power of his stories and characters had only matured along with his basic themes of changing times, changing attitudes, learning from experience, respecting Nature, and the yearning for a simpler, more moderate way of life.

Books are produced in the United States using U.S.-based materials

Books are printed using a revolutionary new process called THINKtech™ that lowers energy usage by 70% and increases overall quality

Books are durable and flexible because of Smyth-sewing

Paper is sourced using environmentally responsible foresting methods and the paper is acid-free

Center Point Large Print

600 Brooks Road / PO Box 1
Thorndike, ME 04986-0001 USA

(207) 568-3717

**US & Canada:
1 800 929-9108**
www.centerpointlargeprint.com